NOEL VIRTUE

THE REDEMPTION OF ELSDON BIRD

PETER OWEN
London and Chester Springs

PETER OWEN PUBLISHERS
73 Kenway Road, London SW5 0RE

Peter Owen books are distributed in the USA by
Dufour Editions Inc., Chester Springs, PA 19425–0007

First published in Great Britain 1987
© Noel Virtue 1987
This paperback edition published 2003

ISBN 0 7206 1166 0

A catalogue record for this book is available from
the British Library

Printed and bound in Great Britain by
Bookmarque Ltd, Croydon, Surrey

To
Marion Benton of New Zealand,
Michael J. Yeomans of England,
and
James Purdy of America,
with love and affection

1 Aunt Melva

The day Elsdon Bird found the dead baby began no differently from any other. He got out of bed in the morning after having been yelled out to a few times. His dad didn't speak to him at the kitchen table. His mum kept grinning at him over her shoulder from where she stood in front of the oven, and the chooks hadn't laid again but Mum said she didn't really mind, the weather was so cold the poor little tykes neded a rest. It was winter.

Elsdon didn't like living in this house. He could remember the one they'd had at Oriental Bay, right near the beach. That had been beaut. He'd gone down to the beach every morning before breakfast collecting firewood for Mum. Sometimes he'd taken yesterday's bread for the gulls. The memory made him jittery. They'd blamed him when the fire destroyed the house. He'd told them over and over he'd never started it. He reckoned his mum believed him. Dad hadn't said either way but he was pretty shook about it. They had lived with Aunt Biddy for a while in Lower Hutt until they were relocated to Waiwhetu Road. It was a real long road with a school at one end and people called Daniels on one side and a madwoman on the other. She wore footy jerseys and sometimes boots, and he'd seen her clomping about in the back yard after it was dark. Mum had told him never to climb over into her yard, which was full of gorse and rusty old billies.

When Dad had left for work Elsdon's mum made him some cocoa for a shout and told him they were going to

Aunt Melva's for the day. 'She's been feeling a bit crook, Elsdon,' she told him.

Elsdon didn't love Aunt Melva, yet he didn't hate her either. She wasn't his aunt but his mum's, and very old. She lived a few miles away near the golf-course. She lived on her own apart from Snowy, her cat. Snowy had one yellow eye and one blue eye and looked just as old as Aunt Melva.

Aunt Melva didn't like children. Elsdon's mum had told him that so many times he never doubted the fact. When they went to visit he would go over to the golf-course as soon as he could escape. There he would search for tees. He had seven now, in a tin under his bed. He always hoped he would find some balls, but he never did.

They left the house as soon as he'd finished his cocoa and walked up the road to where the tram stopped. It was bitterly cold. 'My knees are purple,' Elsdon muttered. Like other boys he was forced to wear shorts even in winter, and hated it. There were a lot of things Elsdon hated. Of course there were a lot of things he liked too. Travelling on the tram was one. Even if the wooden slats dug into your knees when you looked out the window. Mum disapproved of his kneeling on the seats, but this morning she didn't say anything and just sat there after they'd got on, staring at her hands. A few of the women were talking to each other. He knew Mum wouldn't join in because she was pretty shy when Dad wasn't around. One of the women gave him a lolly and patted him on the head. 'What a dear boy you have,' she said in a flash voice. 'So well behaved!'

When his mum was looking the other way Elsdon poked his tongue out at the woman, but she simply smiled back and nodded. Elsdon thought she must be blind. He poked his tongue out again and again to test his thought until the

2

woman looked away with a frown. Elsdon felt a bit bothered at what he had done.

The tram trundled down Waiwhetu Road and turned right at the school, heading towards the shops. Elsdon peered forward eagerly, to see how far away the bridge was. He knew the river would be high, as there'd been lots of rain. The river was always flooding on to the road, which was a beaut sight if there were cars parked along it. The river was the highlight of the trip. Worth putting up with Aunt Melva, who ignored him when she wasn't being grumpy.

The tram stopped in the middle of the bridge. Elsdon stared down at the water. The level was high, as he'd expected. Not quite overflowing the bank but almost. It made him hope the tram would remain there until the water flooded across the road. Down the river came huge branches, what looked like an old tyre, and along the water's edge lay long planks of wood from the factory closest to the bank.

At first when he saw the man's head Elsdon thought it was an oddly shaped footy ball someone had forgotten to take home. It lay in the shallows. When it moved and looked up towards him Elsdon realized that it was a man's head. It was covered with mud. It wasn't until two arms appeared that Elsdon saw it was a whole man struggling to get out of the water. He sneaked a look round the tram. No one else seemed to have noticed. The women were still yacking nineteen to the dozen. His mum was listening, a grin on her face. Elsdon wriggled, moving his knees. He looked back at the man as the tram began to move. The planks of wood, waterlogged and heavy, churned about in the water. In the swift current one of them up-ended and crashed down on to the man's head. He disappeared beneath the surface. Elsdon blinked. Still no one seemed to have noticed. He shook his mum's arm and said, 'There's a

3

bloke in the drink', to which his mum whispered, 'Don't be silly, Elsdon' and frowned at him. She was busy digging into her bag and didn't say anything else.

The tram gathered speed, moving off the bridge and careering down towards the shops. Elsdon turned round and sat quietly on the seat. He knew he hadn't been silly. He had really seen a man in the water but knew enough to realize that no one would believe him, even his mum. For a few minutes he wondered who the man was, who he might have been. He was more curious than upset. He reckoned the man had been killed by the plank falling on him and imagined the body being dragged down to the sea, perhaps floating down to the Antarctic and being found by an explorer, who would write to the dead man's mum and tell her. Then his thinking stopped. He examined the deep lines left on his knees by the slats of the wooden seats. He picked at a scab.

His mum slapped him on the wrist. 'Don't pick,' she said.

He stared up at her. Normally she would chat to him all the way, but today seemed different. He didn't know why. He thought she might be a bit shook about Aunt Melva, who was crook. He didn't know if he cared about Aunt Melva feeling crook. Maybe she would die and he'd be allowed to take Snowy back home with him in a box. Then he felt real bothered about having such thoughts and bit on his tongue.

Elsdon sat very still and thought about the man in the water. Now they had left the bridge behind he wasn't too sure that he had seen anyone at all. Blokes just didn't go swimming in the winter, he told himself. He began to glance up at his mum, wondering if he should tell her again. Perhaps she hadn't heard him right. When he'd stared at her for a long time she noticed him. 'I don't want you bothering Aunt Melva when we get there,' she said. 'You're to be a good boy. She's very old.'

4

'Why doesn't she like me?' he asked.

For a while his mum was silent. Then she frowned. 'She's just real old, Elsdon. Old and tired. She's had a rough life.'

Elsdon knew this hadn't answered his question and told her so. He thought his mum would wallop him one she looked so wild. Then she sighed. 'It's not just you, son. She has never liked kiddies around her. None of us have ever known why. You just have to remember to be good.'

After a few minutes of silence Elsdon realized that his mum wasn't going to say anything more. He twisted round in the seat, staring down the tram. It was moving slowly along the narrow street towards the tram-shed. They were almost there.

When they reached the house his mum was out of breath and stood leaning against the gate. Elsdon stared at the golf-course, wondering how soon he'd be allowed to go over there. The grass looked muddy, but he wouldn't mind that. 'If you're a good boy,' his mum told him, 'you can go over for a while and play.'

His mum had been watching him. As they walked up the path it began to rain and she hurriedly opened the door. She had her own key. Without waiting for him she went straight through into the kitchen. He heard her going out the back. When he looked she was half running down the yard to the clothes-line, collecting the peg-bag as she went. Elsdon knew she wouldn't expect him to help. Getting in the washing was woman's work. His dad had told him that. Aunt Melva would be somewhere upstairs. Sometimes they wouldn't see her for a whole hour after they got there. Sometimes she wouldn't even say good-day when she came downstairs but just start moaning about something that had happened. Last time it had been about the dustman who wouldn't take away any newspapers because she hadn't tied them into a bundle.

He sat quietly at the kitchen table, hands folded, waiting for his mum to come back inside. The rain had stopped. He could hear the clock on the mantelpiece ticking. It sounded like a heart beating. Close by, a fly was buzzing. It was hanging about near the safe door, which reminded him that he was hungry. He got up and looked out through the window. His mum was leaning on the fence talking to Mrs Matu, the old Maori lady next door. Elsdon opened the safe and peered in, wrinkling his nose. Aunt Melva had never used a fridge. Once his dad had brought one over and installed it, but when Mum had visited a week later the fridge was sitting out in the back yard. Aunt Melva kept all her food in the safe. The blowflies loved that. Now, in winter, the smell wasn't too bad. Elsdon opened the biscuit tin and helped himself to three bran slices. Checking that his mum was still yacking with Mrs Matu, he shut the safe door and left the kitchen, heading for the stairs.

He started to feel a bit excited. He had never been in the upper part of the house and knew his mum hadn't either, not for years. Aunt Melva wouldn't let anyone up there. Elsdon was a bit nervy that she would come out from one of the rooms and catch him half-way up, but he saw Snowy watching from the top and forgot about feeling nervy. He'd go on up and have a good gizzo before Mum came inside. If Aunt Melva caught him, he'd say he was just looking for Snowy who'd been making a racket. That'd sound good. Besides, he wouldn't be making a mess and his mum wouldn't have to know if he kept an eye out for her as soon as he'd got up there. He should be able to see her from the windows in one of the rooms. He chewed on a bran slice, putting the others in his pocket.

It got quieter as he climbed. There were queer smells,

like stuff Mum gave him when he had a crook tummy. There was a smell of wee, which made him want to giggle. Aunt Melva usually smelled of wee whenever she gave him a hug, which she did sometimes when his mum had cooked a cake and made Elsdon give it to her.

'Enough to make a bloke sick,' he said to himself. That sounded good, so he said it again. His dad was always saying it when he was reading the newspaper after tea. 'Enough to make a bloke sick.'

Something above him rustled. He stopped, nearly at the top. He listened. There it was again, a noise like paper rustling. Just as he reached the dark, dusty hall and looked along it he saw a small thing running away from him. It looked like a mouse. Snowy wasn't anywhere in sight. All the doors along the hall were shut. The only light came from the far end where there were two small windows. The windows had coloured glass in them. He stared into the gloom, not seeing anything at all. He opened the first door on the right and peered in. It was empty. There were old rag rugs on the floor and a patch of damp in the corner. The room smelled even more strongly of wee. He shut the door and tiptoed down the hall, listening at each door. There were no more sounds.

Right at the end, on the left, leading upward, was a narrow staircase. Sitting on the first step was Snowy, watching him. Elsdon grinned and waved but the cat arched its back, miaowed and ran off. Elsdon followed. It was almost pitch-black up the steps. There didn't seem to be any light switches he could find with his hands. When he reached the top he stood quite still. He'd emerged into an attic room the likes of which he had never seen before. 'Crikey,' he said, again copying his dad. 'A bloke wouldn't credit it.'

He listened. Everything was so still and smelled of dust. A faint light came through a small window under the eaves. His mouth dropped open and he said 'Crikey' again. He felt very bothered. He didn't think he should be up there. Inside the thought he could see his mum giving him a hard walloping if she caught him. He knew that she would get real wild. It was too late to go back down and face Mum and pretend he hadn't seen anything. She would know he had been up to something just by looking at him. She didn't miss much.

The attic was filled with dolls. China dolls, rag dolls, dolls in prams, dolls in cots. They were lying on the floor, propped up in the rafters, bundled together in corners. Each one seemed to be staring at him. Elsdon stood there unable to leave. His eyes met the eyes of the dolls, watching him. Over to the left, half concealed in shadow, sat Snowy. Beside the cat, on a straw pallet, lay Aunt Melva. Her eyes, like the eyes of the dolls, were open. Elsdon took a step back, nearly tripping on the narrow stairwell. He thought he had stopped breathing and had to feel under his blazer for his heartbeat. 'Oh yeah, you're up here, Aunt Melva,' he managed to say.

She didn't answer. She was staring up at the rafters. Elsdon knew that she was dead.

He didn't feel nervy, he was very brave. Stepping carefully, he went across to her and sat down, peering into her eyes. Then he took her hand and held it. It was quite warm. 'My knees got all purple on the way,' he told her. 'It was blinking cold, I can tell you. A bloke wouldn't credit it.'

Then, after he had held her hand up close to his face, studying her fingernails, he said, 'Mum's out the back, getting in the washing. She's having a good old yarn with Mrs Matu. I don't suppose she knows you're dead and gone. She told me not to bother you once we got here. It's enough to make a bloke sick the way she carries on. Dad says that all the time. She said you never liked kiddies.

8

Must have been wrong, what with all these blinking dolls up here and your dead baby.' And he pointed at it.

When he stopped talking, Snowy moved closer and rubbed himself against their joined hands.

Beside Aunt Melva sat an oblong box. It had a hinged lid and a small catch, which Elsdon pushed at with his other hand. When the catch was free he lifted the lid. The flat area on top was made of glass, which was how he had seen the dead baby straight away. Now with the lid open he could see more clearly. In swaddling-clothes grey with age the baby was not much more than a skeleton. Elsdon had never seen a skeleton before but knew it was a real one and from pictures he had looked at in books. Slowly he stretched out and placed his hand on top of the skull, patting it, removing his hand after a long moment. 'A bloke wouldn't credit it,' he said.

Beside him, Snowy had stuck his leg out and was licking it.

From downstairs Elsdon could hear his mum's voice. He reckoned she must be calling for him. He stood up, letting go of Aunt Melva's hand. 'I'll be back soon, I reckon,' he said. 'Don't you fret.'

From the top of the steps he looked back to grin at Aunt Melva. He reckoned the baby must have been hers, that it must have died long ago and she'd kept it up here hidden away so that no one would come and take it from her. In Elsdon's logic, that was a bit of a beaut thing to do. Boy, his mum would be wild.

'I was calling you, Elsdon,' his mum said as he entered the kitchen. She was sitting at the table, a steaming teapot in front of her. The safe door was open, he noticed. In the corner on one of the chairs sat the washing, neatly folded.

'I was with Aunt Melva,' Elsdon told his mum. 'She's up in the attic.'

9

His mum's face went white. She stared at him, watching his face as if there was something in it she didn't want to see. 'Is she coming down?' she asked. Her voice was almost a whisper. It trembled.

Elsdon shuffled from one foot to the other. Now he was in his mum's gaze his feeling of being bothered had returned. From her eyes, before they fully left his, a kind of terror was passed to him. 'Aunt Melva's gone to heaven,' he said.

As they went together up the stairs he reached out and took her hand and held it tightly. He wanted to tell her about the dead baby, but couldn't. Looking upward his mum began to make tiny whimpers of sound. By the time they had reached the upper hall and were moving along it towards the attic steps tears were running down her face.

'No worries, Mum,' Elsdon said loudly, as they began to climb. He drew back his shoulders and stuck out his chest and deepened his voice just like his dad. 'Must have been dead for donkey's years,' he added.

2   Before the Storm

A short time after Aunt Melva had been buried Elsdon's mum suffered her worst attack of asthma.

Elsdon fretted over the dead baby. No one would mention it, nor answer questions about its fate. The questions caused his mum to become so silent he began to wonder if she might be losing her voice. 'No worries, Mum,' he began to tell her. 'She'll be right.'

Whenever he spoke his mum looked at him as if she somehow didn't want him there to remind her. Elsdon knew his mum's opinion of what Aunt Melva had done, despite her having died. It had been a crime. A wicked, sinful act of shame. In her eyes Elsdon could see fear. He didn't understand that, and it bothered him.

Aunt Melva's burial had taken place a few days after Elsdon found her. He hadn't been allowed to go, of course. Mrs Daniels from next door came over to look after him while his mum and dad went off in a black car. His mum wept loudly. His dad was white and silent. The neighbours watched, gossiping together.

They had returned after two hours. Mrs Daniels went home and Elsdon sat at the table while his mum made tea before going to the bedroom without eating a thing. His dad disappeared out to the back yard shed and shut himself in. Elsdon ate his tea.

An article appeared in the *New Zealand Herald*, on the third page. There was a photograph of Aunt Melva as a young woman. Everything was revealed for all the world to read. Nothing was left out.

'Crikey,' Elsdon whispered when he saw the photograph. They had the newspaper delivered, he was up early and he knew his mum and dad would be real wild when they saw it. He left the newspaper on the kitchen table and went out back, climbing over the fence into the big section. It was really a park, an expanse of land people played on. He stood staring at the houses opposite, expecting to see pointing fingers and faces at windows. No one was about. He began to trail across the frost-covered grass, dragging his feet, leaving tracks. He could feel the damp seeping into his gumboots through the holes. 'A bloke wouldn't credit it,' he said loudly to himself.

After ten minutes he felt jittery, reckoned he'd better go back. He'd hide the newspaper in the shed, pretend it hadn't come, but once he was outside the kitchen door he could hear sounds inside, his mum's ragged breathing, his dad's voice, then her crying out, and when he opened the door the sound battered at him. His mum was sitting on a kitchen chair, the newspaper strewn over the floor at her feet. She was still in her nightie. Her face was purple. Dad was leaning over her, trying to make her sit up straight. He didn't turn round when Elsdon entered. Both of them ignored him. Elsdon hurried over to his mum's side and held on to her arm tightly. 'Enough to make a bloke sick,' he said, glaring down at the newspaper.

'Go to your room,' his dad said without looking at him. Elsdon went.

After the doctor had been and gone his dad brought him a cup of cocoa.

'Your mum will be all right, son. She's feeling pretty crook, though. It's the shock you see, son, the shock. It's all a bit much for her.'

Then he left without having looked Elsdon in the face.

Neighbours came and went. Although Elsdon would have liked to join in, he had to stay in his room reading his *Radio Fun* annual and sorting out new pieces of Meccano his dad had brought home. They had the radio on all the time and even though he tried hard he couldn't hear what the neighbours were saying. The only person he saw was Uncle Bryce, who came into his room one afternoon. Elsdon liked Uncle Bryce, his mum's younger brother. They didn't see enough of him, in Elsdon's opinion. He and Uncle Bryce would play for hours sometimes, building things with the Meccano. Elsdon knew his dad didn't like him and often wondered why. Once he asked Uncle Bryce, who went red in the face and shook his head without answering.

'What happened to the dead baby?' Elsdon asked as soon as Uncle Bryce had sat down on the end of the bed. The rest of the house was quiet. Elsdon's mum was having a lie-down and his dad had gone off to a prayer meeting. When both of them went together Mrs Daniels came over to look after Elsdon. He was hoping that his uncle could come and look after him instead.

'The baby was buried with Aunt Melva,' his uncle told him.

'Was it her baby? I reckon it was. Boy, Mum bawled her eyes out when she saw it. She made herself real crook she bawled so much. Snowy must have runned off.'

'No one knows whose baby it was, mate,' Uncle Bryce said.

Elsdon was quiet for only a moment.

'Aunt Melva was a bit of a loony, I reckon. Didn't like her much, but Mum liked her.'

Uncle Bryce didn't talk to Elsdon a lot when he visited,

13

but he never failed to answer Elsdon's questions. The only ones he wouldn't answer were questions about himself. Elsdon knew that Uncle Bryce had never married, that he lived alone somewhere in Wellington near the zoo. He hadn't been allowed to visit his house, but Elsdon always hoped he might, one day. Uncle Bryce was beaut. Secretly Elsdon loved him more than he loved his dad, who never hugged him or played games with him the way Uncle Bryce did.

'You've got some new Meccano,' Uncle Bryce said while he rolled a smoke.

'That's right,' Elsdon replied. 'Dad got it from up the shops in Epuni. Want to help me make something?'

Uncle Bryce shook his head, then handed Elsdon the rolled smoke. Elsdon liked to lick the paper and watch as his uncle carefully finished it off. He would always give a big grin and ruffle Elsdon's hair.

'You're a good little mate,' Uncle Bryce would say. 'A little beauty.'

Elsdon's dad worked in a factory that made car batteries. He was a supervisor. He had never kept the same job for more than a year, but he had always left of his own accord, finding some fault with each place. He was forever trying to save the people he worked with.

'They don't like him very much, Elsdon,' his mum had once told him. 'He keeps on handing out tracts to the sinful and asking them to be born again.'

After Aunt Melva's death they began to go to the Gospel Hall again, twice each Sunday. Elsdon was too young for Bible class. He sat with his mum on one side of the Hall, while his dad sat with the rest of the men on the other. They had to sit there in silence. No one was allowed to play music for hymns on the organ until the evening meeting.

14

Elsdon knew his mum didn't like going very much but she never told him that. He knew it was she who had stopped them going for a long time. Aunt Melva's dying caused the change. One of the Brethren had come round and told them they mustn't backslide any more or else they would go to Hell like Aunt Melva had.

At the morning meeting an old bloke would stand up and read aloud a passage from the Bible, or another might stand up and ask them to sing a certain hymn. None of the women were allowed to stand up at all. Sometimes no one got up for ages and they would all sit in silence.

'You're supposed to think about the Lord and your sins,' Elsdon's mum told him one day when he asked why they sat there for so long with no one doing anything. Then she'd grinned.

Most of the time at the meetings Elsdon stared at the older boys who sat with the men. They would pull faces, trying to make each other giggle. Twice Elsdon had giggled and he'd been given hidings for that when they'd got home. His dad would shut him in his room with the door locked and after an hour would come in with the leather strop he used to sharpen his razor and hit him across the legs and bottom with it, telling him that it was punishment from the Lord.

Sometimes there'd be Communion and those meetings would go on for ever, in Elsdon's opinion. He wasn't allowed to have Communion because he wasn't saved and, crikey, did he get hungry when the loaf of bread was passed round on the plate. The adults would pinch off a small piece and eat it while he was supposed to sit there and understand that it was Jesus's body they were eating. The bread made his tummy rumble. After the bread a large glass of wine was passed round. The wine was supposed to be Jesus's blood, but really it was raspberry juice and his mum would wipe the edge with a hanky before she took a sip. She let it touch her lips only. Elsdon never saw her swallow anything.

No one else on his mum's side of the family went to the Gospel Hall. All his dad's relatives went. His dad's sister Aunt Biddy, who had never married, went to a Gospel Hall in Wellington. Then there was Uncle Judah, his dad's brother, and his wife, Aunt Una. They lived up north in Masterton and were very strict.

Uncle Bryce didn't go to any church and once told Elsdon that on Sundays he went to his best mate's house at Titahi Bay and got shickered on beer. Elsdon pined for the day when he might be allowed to join them.

There was Uncle Bill, Mum's elder brother, and Auntie Vida, his wife. They lived in Petone. Uncle Bill was a tram-driver with huge hands and was six foot three inches tall. He drank beer too and loved his smokes. He called Elsdon's dad 'the little squirt', but not to his face. Elsdon felt a very special feeling for Auntie Vida. She was Irish and had come out from County Cork with her parents when she was a young girl. Sometimes Elsdon was allowed to go and stay with them. He would sit in the huge, steaming kitchen and watch Auntie Vida scrubbing veges at the sink or making a banana cake. She would tell him stories about her girlhood in Ireland and sing songs that had queer words which made Elsdon giggle. Elsdon grew to love Auntie Vida with a sharp pang of need. To him she would have been the best sort of mum a bloke could have. She made life seem fun and warm and filled with a feeling that he was special. Uncle Bill loved her so much he built things in the house just for her. They had a modern telephone, so he made a hatch between the dining-room and hall so she could answer it easily from either place. He put lights above the sink so she would have no worries seeing while she was getting tea ready and scrubbing veges.

16

The three of them would sit at the table for smoko, Uncle Bill always laughing at what she was saying as he rolled a smoke from his tin. They would eat banana cake, and sometimes Elsdon would be allowed to sip Uncle Bill's beer.

'You're a fine, wee chappie,' his Auntie Vida would tell him. 'If only you were my own.'

They hadn't had any kiddies. Uncle Bill had been married before and was divorced. He had a son called Jack. Jack was in the Navy. He never came to see Uncle Bill and had written to say he never would.

Elsdon's dad thought Uncle Bill was a bad sinner. Elsdon once overheard him telling that to his mum.

'He's a bit of all right to me, I reckon,' Elsdon would tell himself when he was alone. 'They both are. I wish Auntie Vida could be my mum.'

When the scandal of Aunt Melva's death had all but faded away and Elsdon was back at school, certain changes took place. His dad was given the sack from work. Elsdon had been indoors that day after school because it was bucketing down outside and his gumboots had holes in them.

'You're to stay in, Elsdon,' his mum told him.

'You said I could go over and feed Mrs Daniels' chooks,' Elsdon moaned.

'Your jersey's soaked through, you need new gumboots, I'm not having you going over there today. You can help me scrub the veges for your dad's tea if you like.'

Elsdon stared out at the darkening day. 'Enough to make a bloke sick,' he mumbled, darting out of the way of his mum's hand. Her attempted slap missed and he ran off into his room, slamming the door.

'There's no point in having a paddy, you're not going

out! You'll get a real hiding when your dad gets home!' his mum shouted after him.

An hour later he heard his dad in the porch stamping his feet on the mat, then the slam of the front door. It was only minutes after when he heard the thump on the floor and his dad's voice shouting for him. For a while he was too scared to leave his room. When he did and peered round the edge of the kitchen door his mum was lying on the lino, her face all purple and twisted. She could hardly breathe. His dad was trying to roll her on to her back and she was moaning. When he saw Elsdon his dad came over to him, took him roughly by the shoulders and stared him in the eyes.

'Your mum's real crook, Elsdon. I've just given her some news and she's taken it bad. I want you to run over to the Daniels and ask them to ring the doctor right away.'

Elsdon ran. Rain fell in a torrent. The sky was as black as pitch. Forked lightning cracked across the sky and the storm seemed to shake the earth around him. Elsdon fell over in the mud trying to climb the fence into the Daniels' section. When he'd got over, he fell again and, struggling to his feet, he thought the wind was trying to lift him off the ground it was so strong. He ran across the grass, ran like blazes towards the Daniels' back door.

'Mum's sick, Mum's sick!' he yelled out. He couldn't find the door and thumped on the wall of the house with his fists. In a terrified voice he added, 'Oh heck, she's going to blinking die!'

3 Ngaire Nation

Elsdon was staring through the gap in the Mad Woman's hedge. It was early morning, not yet fully light. His dad was asleep. Across the grass of the section behind him lay a heavy frost. Elsdon was wearing his gumboots.

The Mad Woman, whose name was Ngaire Nation, was staring back at him from the steps leading up to the fly-screen door of her house.

Elsdon spoke loudly. 'My mum's crook,' he said. 'They took her off in a ambulance. She could be dead soon, I reckon.'

The Mad Woman stared at him without expression. A fat black cat was curling round her feet, placing its paws delicately on the Rugby boots she was wearing.

'You wouldn't credit it,' Elsdon said even more loudly. Then he added, 'What's the name of your cat?'

The Mad Woman's lips began to move. 'I know who you are, little boy. You've come to steal the balls.'

'No I haven't,' Elsdon said. He tried to look concerned and asked, 'Whose balls are they?'

'They belong to Jesus,' the Mad Woman told him.

'Can I come in there and see them?'

Ngaire Nation adjusted her jersey. It was so long it reached half-way down her legs, partly covering the stained strides she wore underneath. The jersey was black with a white collar. On the left side in front was stitched a silver fern. Elsdon reckoned it must be an All Blacks jersey.

He hadn't seen one before and hoped she might let him have it if he talked nicely to her.

The Mad Woman was beckoning him with her hand. He pushed his way through the gap in the hedge, through the waist-high weeds to where she waited on the steps. The cat had gone, running off under the house.

'You've got veges growing there,' Elsdon said helpfully, pointing them out. Along the outer skirting were several seeded cabbages and a row of drooping runner beans.

The Mad Woman took no notice. Elsdon followed her up the steps.

Ngaire Nation had been collecting footballs for as many years as Elsdon had been alive. She was well known in the district. Harmless, she was watched over by nurses from the Plunket Society, who out of kindness visited her once a week. Where the balls came from no one knew, although children sometimes claimed to have lost them. Where her obsession had begun, nobody was sure. It had always been that way.

It was thought by others in the road that she'd had a son, killed at Gallipoli, who had played Rugby and would have been an All Black had he survived the wicked war. Most accepted that theory, for it explained everything. Times being as they were, she was let to live her life the way she wanted. She harmed no one. Ngaire Nation was the Mad Woman and no one questioned it or did anything to change it. At least, that's how it had been.

Elsdon's mum had been at the hospital in Lower Hutt for three days. She had suffered a mild heart attack, brought on by shock, and asthma.

'We'll be on our own for a while,' Elsdon's dad told him. 'The doctor's a good bloke, but she's real sick this time.'

He didn't say that she might die. Elsdon reckoned he

could see that thought in his eyes, though. A look of fear.

'You're to stay home from school,' his dad told him. 'I've rung the headmaster.'

Elsdon hated school. It was beaut to stay home. School was crud. The teachers were always telling him off for butting in and asking questions when he wasn't supposed to. They didn't want him to learn. How could he learn if he didn't ask questions? It was stupid.

When the ambulance had arrived for Mum the darkening day was so stormy Elsdon was more nervy of the thunder than of what was going on inside the house. Two blokes in uniform carried Mum out through the front door, a blanket wrapped round her. His dad held her hand, walking alongside. Elsdon followed. By the time they had got out on to the road where the ambulance was parked, some of the neighbours were standing round watching, whispering amongst themselves. Elsdon had felt pretty important for a couple of minutes. When rain began to bucket down he ran back inside, then remembered he hadn't said tata to Mum. He sat down at the table, his chin cupped in his hands. 'Mum could die, I reckon,' he said loudly. But he couldn't hear himself above the storm.

He didn't know his dad was going to the hospital with Mum until Mrs Daniels came in the back door all wet and dripping. 'You poor little tyke,' she said. 'I'll make a drink.'

'I'd like cocoa, please,' Elsdon told her.

Mrs Daniels came over and tweaked his cheek. 'You can have what you like!' she said, grinning down at him.

Elsdon stared at the hairs on her upper lip and hoped she wouldn't hug him. She always smelled of onions.

'Your dad's gone off with your mum,' Mrs Daniels told him. 'He'll be back later on. After your cocoa you can get into bed and I'll read you a story.'

'I like *Radio Fun*,' Elsdon said. 'I've got a new one Dad

got me. There's a story in it about a lady spy called Mrs Fields.'

'That sounds beaut to me,' Mrs Daniels said.

She had stayed with him all night and his dad had come home the next morning looking real crook.

The Mad Woman's fly-screen door slammed shut behind them. The noise made Elsdon feel nervy. The kitchen was gloomy and it was a while before his eyes could see much. 'Crikey,' he whispered, when they did. 'A bloke wouldn't credit it.'

The Mad Woman was getting a bottle of milk out of the safe. She poured some into a jar, which Elsdon recognized as once containing peanut butter. The jar had red and yellow stripes. Elsdon kicked off his gumboots and sat down, taking the jar of milk. 'Ta,' he said, not knowing what else to say. 'I'm pretty keen on milk.'

'A cow gives us milk,' the Mad Woman said. 'God gives us cows.'

'Yeah, we're lucky, I reckon.'

Ngaire Nation stood watching as Elsdon drank. When he had finished, she leaned forward. With her thumb she gently wiped away the excess drops that had collected on Elsdon's upper lip. Then she nodded and patted him on the head. 'You are one of God's kiddies,' she said.

'My dad's called Len,' Elsdon told her, 'and my mum's crook at the moment. She might be pushing up the daisies soon. I'll have to look after Dad, he can't cook or anything but I can. I s'pose I'll have to stay home from school for donkey's years.'

Ngaire Nation didn't speak, she just looked at him. At that moment three ancient cats walked into the kitchen. They settled at Elsdon's feet and immediately began to purr.

'Blimey,' said Elsdon, 'you've got a lot of cats. Do you have names for all of them?'

'There's Joseph and Mary, Ruth and Paul. There was Jehovah but he died, poor thing. Paul's outside.'

'Do you know my name?' Elsdon asked.

'God's kiddies need no names,' said the Mad Woman.

Elsdon felt a bit bothered. 'My name's Elsdon,' he said.

In the silence that followed, Elsdon stared about the room. It was huge. He had never seen such clutter, everywhere he looked. Hanging from hooks in the ceiling, resting on shelves, dozens of various coloured footy jerseys and black boots filled the kitchen, along with stacks of newspapers so high they threatened to topple over. A large number of the jerseys were like the one the Mad Woman was wearing. All Blacks jerseys, with the silver fern. The boots were caked with dried mud and most were without laces. Yet the kitchen smelled sweet with the scent of ripening apples. A moist, warm smell which Elsdon thought was a bit of all right. He looked across at the Mad Woman and grinned. She grinned back. 'Your mum's crook?' she asked.

'Oh yeah, she's real sick. She's in the hospital. Dad says she might be in there for a heck of a long time, but he's not sure. It isn't the same with her not here. Dad's kept me home from school. He's not at work any longer, he got the boot, and Mrs Daniels has been making my lunch. Aunt Melva died and so did her baby and I wanted to have Snowy, but Dad said he prob'ly has runned away so we won't be having him, I reckon.'

When he finished talking he felt sick and leaned with his elbow on the table, his chin cupped in his hand. He felt like having a bawl, but then thought he was just excited being in the Mad Woman's house. He had been waiting for her to be mad, but she hadn't been. He liked her.

'I think your jerseys and footy boots are real neat,' he

23

said, hoping that she might offer him the jersey he now wanted so much.

Ngaire Nation frowned. 'You haven't come to take your ball back, have you?' she asked.

'I haven't got a ball,' Elsdon told her politely.

'I think you've come here to steal,' the Mad Woman said. She stared at him with widened eyes.

'No I haven't. My mum said that anyone who steals will be put into Hell when they die,' Elsdon said in a matter-of-fact voice. 'When I get old I shall get saved, and then even if I do steal I'd still go up to live with Jesus.' He felt a bit silly saying that, and grinned.

'There's no such place,' said Ngaire Nation. 'Everywhere's Hell.'

Elsdon had finished his milk. She had refilled the jar and he'd drunk it all. He put the jar down on the table and bent to stroke one of the cats. 'Crikey, I wouldn't steal,' he said quietly. 'Only cruds steal. I'm not a crud, I reckon.'

He didn't want the Mad Woman to think him bad, as she might not offer him a jersey.

When the face appeared, squinting through the fly-screen door, neither Elsdon nor Ngaire Nation noticed.

The face remained there, watchful, for several minutes before it spoke. 'Elsdon,' it said very loudly. 'You're to get home straight away. Your dad wants to take you to see your mum. I've been looking all over the place for you.'

The face withdrew. It had been Mrs Daniels.

'Oh heck,' Elsdon grizzled. 'If Dad sent her over, then he must be raring to go. If I don't get a move on he'll be in a paddy and I might get a hiding. He doesn't give me hidings very much, but when he does it makes my bum real sore.'

He began to pull on his gumboots, watching the Mad

24

Woman's back. She had turned away when she'd seen Mrs Daniels, becoming still like a wild rabbit when it is cornered. She didn't speak.

Elsdon stood up and waited, hopefully. He thought she might be about to give him a footy jersey. 'I'm going to go now, lady,' he said.

Ngaire Nation still didn't say anything. She continued to stand with her back to him and the door. There was no movement from her. The cats had walked across the room to join her. They stood at her feet looking up at her with hoity-toity faces.

'You're beaut, Mrs Nation,' Elsdon said in a quiet voice. Then loudly, in case she hadn't heard, he repeated the words, adding, 'If I hear any of the jokers round here slinging off at you I'll butt in and tell them you're my friend and I sure don't reckon you're mad at all even if you do wear footy jerseys and boots.' He almost shouted the word jerseys. He would have liked to go across and give her a hug, but he was too nervy she might show she was mad. Suddenly he wanted a jersey so much he felt his face going red. If he had one of her jerseys he could wear it all the time, even to bed, and when he did the washing-up and when they went to visit Mum and when he walked to school.

The Mad Woman made a half-turn, glanced at his face, then looked away. Elsdon tried to grin.

'I put rat poison in your drink,' she told him.

Elsdon fled.

4   Looking for Snowy

During the weeks his mum was in the hospital Elsdon
thought he saw a man eating a cooked cat.

Before that happened he watched the Mad Woman
being taken away in a truck. There were three blokes in
white coats who did the dirty deed. Elsdon watched it all
from Mum and Dad's bedroom window by standing on the
bed. His dad was out looking for work, so Elsdon knew
that his watching wouldn't be disturbed. He had never
seen anything like it since he'd found the dead baby. The
neighbours were all out on the road having a good look.
Mrs Daniels was there leaning against the letter-box with
Mrs Rahana, a Maori lady who lived in the bush on the
other side of the road. They were yacking away nineteen to
the dozen.

Elsdon had been sitting in front of the radio listening to
Aunt Daisy. He tried to listen to her every morning, if he
could. He would sing along with the words of the song
that was always played before the programme started.
Aunt Daisy's voice was warm and deep and friendly and it
felt like she was really talking to no one else except him. He
had tried to write down the recipes she read out for his
mum, but Aunt Daisy talked very fast and a lot of the
words he couldn't spell anyway.

At first the noises just annoyed him. 'Oh heck, Aunt
Daisy,' he said to her. 'A bloke can't even hear you properly. And I've turned this blinking thing up as high as
it'll go.'

26

He was sitting on the floor, his head against the speakers. The radio stood as tall as he was and towered over him when he sat on the floor. Elsdon liked to look at the egg-shaped dial with the yellow light as he listened. Sometimes he would pick at the material that covered the speakers inside the cabinet, or run his fingers along the shiny wood surface. Once he had seen behind it, when his dad was changing a valve. He loved the radio.

Soon the noises coming from outside were so loud he stood up and looked out back across the big section. There were shouts and then someone moaning. The moaning got louder and became cries.

'Blimey, Aunt Daisy!' Elsdon cried. 'Someone must be getting murdered!'

There was no one in sight out back. When he craned his head and looked to the left he could see a lot of jokers peering through the hedge into Ngaire Nation's yard. It wasn't them making the noise. That seemed to be coming from somewhere out the front. Elsdon ran out of the living-room, across the narrow hall and into his mum and dad's bedroom. Here the noise was at its loudest.

They were taking the Mad Woman away.

Elsdon felt real bothered. Ngaire Nation was lying on her side on a stretcher, trussed up like a chook in a queer-looking white jacket. Her bright red hair was all over the place. He tried to wave to her, to shout out, but he wasn't too sure then what was going on. She was screaming her block off by now and twisting and turning on the stretcher as if she'd had itching powder put down her front like he'd had done once at school.

'Leave her alone!' he shouted at the blokes.

No one heard him because there was so much noise. One other bloke came running down the path now, and when he reached her side the two blokes carrying her put the stretcher on the ground. They did something to her

27

arm and Ngaire Nation fell back on to the stretcher and didn't move again.

'Oh heck, she must be dead!' Elsdon cried. He jumped down from the bed and ran to the front door, yanking it open, about to rush out.

Mrs Daniels saw him and hurried down the path, holding up her hands, trying to shoo him back into the house. 'You better not come out, son. It isn't nice,' she said, reaching the steps.

Elsdon tried to see past her. She was standing in front of him, blocking his view.

'Mrs Nation must be real crook the way she carried on,' Elsdon said. 'Is she dead? I reckon she is, she stopped moving. Why was she wearing that funny jacket? Who were those blokes? I didn't like all that yelling, I was trying to hear Aunt Daisy on the blinking radio,' he said as Mrs Daniels urged him inside, shutting the front door and leading him into the kitchen.

'I'll make some cocoa,' Mrs Daniels said. 'You'd better turn the radio off, son. We can sit in here and have a good yarn. Take your mind off it.'

She was frowning once the jug was on the boil and kept looking over at him. He had sat at the table and was staring at the formica top.

'She was a nice lady, I reckon. I liked her,' Elsdon said, close to tears. 'She didn't really put rat poison in my drink, that was just her joke because she was wild I couldn't stay and see her balls and things. What will happen to her footy jerseys now she's dead?'

'She isn't dead, Elsdon,' Mrs Daniels said softly. 'The hospital orderly gave her something to make her sleep. She's a bit crook in the head.'

'Where'd they take her to?'

'To a special hospital where she'll be happier. She'll be in a mental home, Elsdon. You mustn't be scared of that

word. Poor Mrs Nation is mental. That i.
well in her head and needs looking after. S.
have been living there on her own, it wasn't sa.

'She never bothered anyone. She didn't seem
the head to me. She could've been my friend. A
wouldn't credit it.'

'You mustn't get yourself upset, Elsdon,' Mrs Daniels
said. Then she added brightly, 'Your dad should be home
soon. He might have some good news about a job!' She
brought over his cocoa.

'All this stuff going on,' Elsdon said, not looking at her.
'It makes you feel like going out and getting shickered.'

'Elsdon!' Mrs Daniels said. Then she laughed and
leaned down, putting her arms about him in a hug.

Elsdon began to cry, mostly because the hug gave him a
whiff of Mrs Daniels's onion smell and he'd had enough of
being bothered.

'Poor wee tyke,' Mrs Daniels whispered, patting him on
the head. 'You're a good little chap, Elsdon.'

Elsdon wrote Ngaire Nation's name in his *Radio Fun*
annual, on the back page. He didn't know how to spell her
name, but he would know whose name it was whenever
he looked at it from now on. He felt he had lost someone.

'I didn't know her very well,' he said quietly, 'but she
could've been my friend whatever anyone said. It isn't
right.'

Mrs Daniels had cooked Elsdon's tea and brought over
some old *Phantom* comics for him to read.

'I'd like to stay with you, Elsdon, but Wendy's a bit sick
with a fever. If you need me, son, just shout from the back
door.'

Wendy was her daughter. Elsdon thought Wendy was
hoity-toity. He was pleased Mrs Daniels couldn't stay. It

meant he wouldn't have to go to bed early. Dad would go and see Mum in the hospital before he came home. He wouldn't be back for hours.

'A bit of all right, being on my own,' Elsdon said after Mrs Daniels had gone. 'A bloke needs a bit of peace.'

Elsdon's dad arrived back after dark. He was grinning from ear to ear. Elsdon couldn't believe his eyes when he saw Snowy. The cat was crouched inside a leather bag, the zip pulled over so far only Snowy's head was visible. With his one yellow and one blue eye he stared at Elsdon and hissed.

'Crikey, Dad, where did you find him?' Elsdon asked.

'Over at Aunt Melva's. He hadn't run away after all. Mrs Matu had been giving him feeds. He was living in her wash-house. He's a bit thin, Elsdon. We'll have to take good care of him.'

Elsdon rushed over to hug his dad. His dad backed away. Elsdon stared at the cat.

Because of Snowy's arrival Elsdon forgot his upset over the Mad Woman being taken away to the mental home. Though he asked Mrs Daniels over the fence why the blokes in white coats had been so rough.

'They had to be, Elsdon,' she said, unable to look him in the eye. 'She was very strong. You have to be cruel to be kind.'

Elsdon didn't think that answered his question.

Mrs Daniels hadn't come over that day, as his dad was home. Elsdon knew she didn't like his dad much. They'd had a row once over her chooks making too much of a racket. Elsdon had overheard Mrs Daniels talking to Mrs Rahana. 'He's a cold man, Mrs R, like a dead fish,' she had said. 'I feel real sorry for Elsdon. Lord knows what will happen to the little tyke.'

The cat Snowy was restless. Elsdon had decided he was to be his friend.

'I haven't got any friends, Snowy,' Elsdon told the cat. 'None of the blokes at school are. I thought Mrs Nation might be, but she's been took away. It makes a bloke sick.'

Snowy stared at him from the other side of the room. He had taken to sitting underneath the sideboard and Elsdon had to lie on his tummy to talk, inching closer each time. Elsdon talked and talked. The cat sat crouched down, watching him, his eyes never leaving Elsdon's face. He had been eating lean slices of cold mutton but turned up his nose at the bone Elsdon offered on a tin plate.

'I reckon you miss Aunt Melva,' Elsdon suggested. 'Do you remember when I found the dead baby? That's all over now. Aunt Melva's pushing up the daisies in the cemetery and I think they put the baby in with her. I don't know if it was her baby, no one told me. No one tells me things. I've got to go back to school tomorrow, Dad said, as they're having a test or something and I won't like it. No worries, you're going to be my friend. I'll leave lots of grub for you so you won't have a rumbly tummy. Do you like savaloys? My dad might be out all day today. Mum's in the hospital, she's been crook with a dicky heart.'

Elsdon knew enough not to touch the cat. Snowy was feeling pretty crook too, being humped about in a bag all over the place. Elsdon reckoned he understood Snowy's feelings. 'I like you, Snowy,' he told the cat, 'but you mustn't go outside or you might go over to Mrs Daniels' section and put her chooks off laying. She gets six eggs from them every day. She gave me a chook egg one day and I boiled it in water and ate it with some bread. I like savaloys better than eggs. Mrs Daniels calls eggs googies. You'll like her, I reckon. She's my friend when she's not being hoity-toity. She comes over here quite a bit, but she won't hurt you. She knows all about Aunt Melva and that.'

After school the following day Elsdon ran all the way home and let himself in the back door. The door was never locked and often left wide open when Mum was home. His dad was out again looking for work, and Mrs Daniels was supposed to have been cooking his tea and bringing it over when he got home. Elsdon wasn't too keen on her food. She boiled leeks without salt and grilled sausages until they were so hard they hurt his teeth. For pudding there would always be rhubarb with lumpy custard. Mrs Daniels grew rhubarb all over her back yard. 'Rhubarb is good for you, Elsdon,' Mrs Daniels had told him. 'It helps you go.'

Snowy wasn't under the sideboard. It was the first place Elsdon looked. He ran into the kitchen, having left his school bag on the floor. Mrs Daniels was standing in front of the oven, hanging washing over the clothes-horse. She didn't turn round when he rushed in.

'My friend isn't there,' Elsdon said loudly.

'Your tea will be ready soon, Elsdon,' Mrs Daniels said. She kept her back to him.

Elsdon searched the house. He even peered into the wash-house but didn't really think Snowy could be there. The copper boiler was full of soapy water, and buckets filled with soaking clothes sat on the floor. Mrs Daniels had been doing their washing. She'd spilt Rinso all over the place.

'No one asked her to do the washing,' Elsdon said. 'I reckon she left the blinking door open and she won't tell me. Enough to make a bloke real wild.'

32

Mrs Daniels said she hadn't known about Snowy. 'I've been out the back hanging up the washing,' she told him as Elsdon was trying to push his fork through a sausage. 'I didn't know about the cat, son. I'm sorry. He might have got out.'

'He'll have runned away,' Elsdon said. 'He looked pretty fed up this morning. We were going to be friends. A bloke wouldn't credit it. Aunt Melva would've wanted me to keep Snowy safe.'

After tea Mrs Daniels helped Elsdon to search the back yard. 'You have to look under things,' Elsdon told her, pointing. 'Cats like to hide, I reckon.'

After a few minutes Mrs Daniels gave up. 'I don't think he's here, Elsdon,' she said. 'I think we should hang on until the morning. It'll be dark very soon.'

Elsdon followed her inside. He sat on the settee in the living-room, pretending to read one of the *Phantom* comics until Mrs Daniels had gone. Then he took the big torch from the kitchen and began to hunt for his friend. 'I'll have to find him and make him safe,' he said loudly.

It was dark outside now, but there was a moon. It helped Elsdon from feeling too nervy. He didn't care if his dad came home and he wasn't there. Even if he got a hiding. 'Snowy's more important than an old hiding,' he said.

He looked beneath every bush in the front yard and poked the torch under the house, calling Snowy's name. There was no response, no sign that the cat was anywhere near. Elsdon peered between the concrete posts along Mrs Daniels's fence. He could see her through a window with hoity-toity Wendy. 'Better not go in their yard,' he told himself. 'Prob'ly scare the chooks. If Snowy was over there the chooks would be cackling, I reckon.'

Somehow Elsdon couldn't go into the Mad Woman's section either. He stared through the gaps in the hedge, calling for Snowy.

He had seen Ngaire Nation's cats being carted off in boxes. Mrs Daniels had said they would go to the Pound, a place where cats went when they weren't wanted.

'I would've wanted them,' he told her.

'They were wild beasts,' said Mrs Daniels. 'It's best they went off like that. They smelled, Elsdon.'

Elsdon thought Mrs Daniels was getting more and more hoity-toity, like Wendy was. He didn't like her much any more. 'She's a bit of an old biddy, if you ask me,' he said, like his dad had said once to his mum.

On the other side of Waiwhetu Road, where Mrs Rahana lived in the bush, was the market garden. It was owned by a man in Woburn called by everyone the Moaning Pom. Nobody seemed to like him. He wouldn't be there now. Elsdon decided to cross the road to see if Snowy had gone over and got lost. He knew he'd be in real trouble if he were caught. He looked up and down the road but couldn't see his dad or anyone. He'd shut the back door. Mrs Daniels would think he was reading comics. Holding the lit torch in front of him with both hands, his arms outstretched, Elsdon ran.

To the left of the market garden the bush spread out, most of it gorse and pongas and fern until it began to climb up towards the hills where the trees were. The hills were called the Ranges. The Ranges spread along the skyline all the way to Wellington. Mrs Rahana lived in an old bach in the bush, and some of the blokes at school had told Elsdon that she was a witch.

The market garden gates were never shut at night. Elsdon stopped running when he reached them. He could see no lights on in any of the sheds and it was very quiet. 'I reckon Snowy's over here. He'd come over for a bit of peace away from Mrs Daniels,' he said. He didn't want to call out in case anyone was about.

He walked down the paths, flashing the torch under

everything. Ahead of him, from the bush, he could hear a mopoke. He disturbed a possum that had been feeding on fruit fallen from the rows of trees. Elsdon nearly shouted out in shock. The beam of the torch had made the possum's eyes flash. It hurried off over the fence, back into the bush.

Elsdon came to a gap in the fence and looked through. Over to the right was an old tin shack. It had potato sacks for a door, bricks on the roof holding down the corrugated iron, and around it were cluttered mounds of rotting veges and fruit. There were empty sacks everywhere on the ground. Elsdon could see clearly, as there were lights on inside the shack and a bonfire near the door. Sitting on a wooden box, not looking in Elsdon's direction, sat an old Chinaman. Elsdon had forgotten about him, had heard about Old Chu from a nasty girl at school who said she had chased him one day shouting out rude words. Elsdon crouched down behind the gorse and turned off his torch.

The Chinaman was eating from a tin plate, using his fingers. Elsdon could hear words being muttered, saw the Chinaman lifting up pieces of meat and sliding them into his mouth. From the light of the bonfire Elsdon could see grease all round the Chinaman's mouth. He was gnawing on a bone.

Stretched on the outside wall of the shack, held there by nails, was an animal skin.

Elsdon began to feel a bit crook.

The fur was white.

Without waiting to see anything more, Elsdon stood up and began to run back along the path from where he'd come, holding the torch tightly in his hands. He wanted to shut his eyes but couldn't. His mouth was dry and his eyes had begun to water. Almost at the gate he fell over, landing with a thump on his side.

'Hey boy, what you doing, eh? You come over to get some free grub?'

The voice was very loud. It was Mrs Rahana. She was standing just inside the gate. She held a large stick but was grinning. Elsdon was cold and scared and he wanted his mum. He didn't think he could get past the Maori lady, as she was standing in the way. He tried to tell her what he had seen but the words jumbled in his mouth. Mrs Rahana simply stood and stared and grinned.

Elsdon ran. He ran round her across the road without looking to his right or left, past the letter-box, down the path and into the house. When he was inside he stood in the darkness, listening.

His dad was still out. There was no sign of Snowy.

By the time his dad did get home Elsdon was in bed with the light off. When his dad looked in he pretended to be asleep.

'Snowy's been murdered and eaten,' Elsdon told Mrs Daniels the next morning. He wasn't able to tell his dad. 'It's all your fault. I'm telling on you when Mum gets home.'

Mrs Daniels didn't seem to have heard a word he'd said. She had come over as soon as she'd seen his dad marching off down the road to the railway station. He was going into Wellington on the train. He'd told Elsdon not to worry about Snowy. 'I'm going in to see a man about a job,' he said. 'Mum will be home soon. You mustn't fret.'

Elsdon's eyes had been watering. He didn't tell his dad he was crying about Snowy. His dad told him he could stay home from school if he was feeling a bit crook.

'Snowy was going to be my friend,' Elsdon told Mrs Daniels. 'You left the door open, I reckon, and Snowy runned away. Now he's dead and been eaten. It isn't right.'

Mrs Daniels hadn't known what to say. Her face was red

36

and puffy. 'Wendy's very sick, son,' she said eventually, in a small voice. 'She might have died yesterday if the doctor hadn't come. I was doing your washing to keep my mind off it. The doctor's coming again this morning. Wendy might have to go into the hospital. I'm sorry about your cat. He'll come back, I'm sure of it.'

Elsdon wasn't too aware of what she was saying either, although he thought her voice sounded queer. He could think only about Snowy being dead.

'Will Snowy be up in Heaven now?' he asked her.

'You'll have to ask your dad about that, Elsdon.'

Elsdon was left alone all that day. For a while he played with his Meccano and listened to Aunt Daisy. 'My cat's dead,' he told her. 'He runned away and was eaten by a Chinaman.'

Aunt Daisy was talking about Edmunds' Baking Powder.

'Nobody listens,' Elsdon said loudly, switching the radio off. He decided to go over to the Mad Woman's house and look at her balls and try to find a footy jersey. 'She would've given me one anyway, I reckon,' he told himself. 'Specially now Snowy's been murdered. She wouldn't have liked it if one of her cats was murdered. A bloke wouldn't credit it. I reckon Mrs Daniels wouldn't like it if one of her chooks got out and was knocked on the head and had all its skin taken off and was eaten by a China-man.'

Ngaire Nation's house was locked and boarded up. The windows had been covered with brown paper. Elsdon couldn't even see inside.

'Oh heck, I shall get real shook soon. If Dad had any beer I'd get shickered. That'd show them.'

For a while he tramped around the big section in his

gumboots, wishing that the grassy park on to which all the houses backed had trees or a stream. He crouched down beside the area where games of marbles were played, hoping to find one. But the ground was muddy from rain that had fallen in the night. On the far side he could see some older boys with bikes, riding up and down. 'I could join them, I reckon,' he said, 'but they look like a bunch of bodgies to me. They'll only start slinging off.'

The day seemed to stretch out before him without end. 'Enough to make a bloke sick,' he said.

His dad arrived home for tea. He was carrying something in a sack. Elsdon thought he looked real fed up too.

'Mum sends her love, Elsdon,' he said quietly. Then in an even quieter voice, 'I found Snowy, son. He was lying in the gutter down by the school. He's been run over, son. I shall have to dig a grave in the back yard. Do you want to help?'

Elsdon began to cry. His dad stood watching for a while then he went out through the back door, carrying the sack over his shoulder.

The following days Elsdon wouldn't go into the back yard, wouldn't look out the window. He didn't believe Snowy was buried there. 'The Chinaman ate him,' he kept telling himself.

5   To the Waikato

Elsdon mum didn't die. She was sent home from the hospital four weeks after she went in.

'I prayed for you, Jessie,' Elsdon's dad told her.

She didn't reply and stared at him for a long time.

Elsdon was sitting at the table building a grader from his Meccano set. He wasn't very good at building things but that didn't stop him trying. 'Have a go, Elsdon,' his dad had said. 'Don't want to grow up to be a sissy, do you?'

Elsdon didn't really mind. He played with the Meccano because he was bored. Not allowed to go out the back to the big section and play, told to stay indoors and be quiet. He was real fed up now that Snowy and Mrs Nation were gone. 'Makes a bloke sick, this doing nothing,' he had said to himself earlier. Just because his mum had been crook. Now she was home again he wasn't allowed to do what he liked. He really felt like doing his block and telling them just what he was thinking. Still, at least he was home from school. That was neat. And the way things were going he might never have to go back, a fact he had overheard and thought a bit of all right. They'd had a letter from the school though, moaning about his attendance only on odd days. Of course they didn't let on about that. Mum and Dad seemed to have a lot of secrets lately, but he listened with his ear against their door late at night when they thought he was asleep. 'Learned quite a bit. Anyone would think a bloke didn't have the right to know, the way they carry on.'

One morning when they were alone, Elsdon took his mum's hand and led her out into the back yard. He had told her all about Snowy and how he'd looked for him and about the Chinaman and the white fur skin on the wall and about poor Mrs Nation. 'Dad says Snowy's in that grave,' Elsdon said, pointing at it. 'He dug it. I didn't see, so I'm not sure he's there. Snowy was neat. I talked and talked to him and he listened. I reckon that China bloke knocked him off and ate him for tea.'

'Don't be silly, Elsdon,' his mum said. She wasn't really listening and was staring into the distance across the big section.

They stood there like that for a long time, Elsdon's eyes on the grave and his mum's far off. Suddenly she made a queer noise like a sob and pulled her hand from his, turning away and walking slowly back into the house. Elsdon remained where he was. The sound had scared him a bit.

Things were changing. Elsdon wasn't too keen on the changes. They went to the Gospel Hall twice a week too. Prayer meetings on Wednesday nights and the meeting on Sunday morning. He knew they were thinking about sending him to Sunday school, before the morning meeting. They didn't go there Sunday night because Mum was still feeling a bit rough and needed to go to bed early. His dad said a real long grace before every meal, and his mum kept talking about how he was born again. She had changed most of all and didn't sling off at Dad any more. She had brought out the old Bible and put it on the sideboard and Elsdon had to listen to her reading aloud from it every night.

Elsdon was told he was too young to be saved. Eventually he would be expected to come to the Lord and ask for his sins to be forgiven. Elsdon thought it was pretty stupid, but he had no choice. If his mum and dad were going to belong to the Brethren for good now, he'd just have to like it or lump it.

'You mustn't say the Lord's name, Elsdon,' his mum told him. 'Not until you have been saved. We are all sinners and your dad and me we've been backsliding for a long time. It hasn't been easy for us. With your dad out of work and me being crook, we have had to sacrifice. It will all be better soon.' And she hugged him, held him to her bosom as she had when he was very small.

'I do love you, Mum,' he would tell her.

'I know you do, Elsdon. You must love your dad too and be a good boy. One day all your sins will be washed away, washed in the blood of the Lamb.'

Elsdon at the time was sitting on the bread-bin below the window. His mum was making girdle-scones, cooking them on top of the oven. Elsdon liked to lick out the mixing-bowl. Sometimes his mum would turn on the radio and they would listen to the morning serial, *Doctor Paul*, followed by Aunt Daisy's programme. She told real interesting stories in between the recipes.

'Things aren't the same any more,' Elsdon said.

'How do you mean, Elsdon?' asked his mum.

'Dunno. I think there's too much yacking about Jesus.'

As soon as he'd said it Elsdon felt his face go red and he knew he was in for a hiding. His mum wiped her hands on a tea-towel and before Elsdon knew it he was being dragged across the floor out of the kitchen to his room, his mum not saying anything. She was breathing in a heavy, noisy way and he began to get scared she would have an attack. She pushed him into his room and stood at the door staring at him in anger.

'You will stay here without tea until your dad gets home, do you hear me? You're in for a good hiding. The Lord is very angry at you! I shall pray for you, Elsdon.'

Then she slammed the door and locked it.

Elsdon sat on the edge of the bed. He knew he wouldn't cry, not yet anyway. He might bawl his eyes out when he got his hiding though, for he had all the times before.

Elsdon looked up at the ceiling. 'I bet you wouldn't have a paddy and give me hidings, Jesus,' he said.

His tummy rumbling, Elsdon undressed, put on his pyjamas and got into bed. There were no sounds in the house. He was half asleep when he heard the door being unlocked and opened. His mum stuck her head in and glared at him. 'You're a sinner, Elsdon,' she said quietly. 'It's you who makes me so crook.'

Then she slammed the door, but didn't lock it again.

Elsdon fell asleep sucking his thumb, something he hadn't done since he was a baby. He was not aware of his mum returning to the door every so often. She would open it, stand there glaring, then go away, only to come back a few minutes later. Eventually the room grew dark as the night crept into it. The house remained silent. Elsdon didn't even wake up when his dad came home with the good news.

Elsdon wasn't given the hiding from Dad his mum had threatened. His mum forgot he had been disrespectful to Jesus, as his dad had brought home the news of getting a job. He had been offered a job as manager of a swimsuit factory in Morrinsville, up north in the Waikato. They were to go by car and trailer which Dad had bought with money Uncle Bill loaned them. They had a house to go to. Elsdon would go to a new school.

'Crikey,' Elsdon said when his mum told him the news.

She was so happy it made her forget she was angry at him. 'The Lord looks after His own, Elsdon,' she told him. 'All this is because we have come back into the fold. We are redeemed.'

Elsdon was taken to the Wednesday prayer meeting that night at the Hall in Lower Hutt. An old geezer spoke to Elsdon as they were leaving. He had been staring at him during the meeting with a frown on his face. Elsdon had been making a cat's-cradle with a piece of string. He tied knots in the string too and made faces at some of the snooty boys on the other side of the hall. 'One day you will find salvation,' the old geezer had said. Elsdon thought he must be a bit crook in the head, like Mrs Nation was supposed to be.

'That old boy's a bit of an old biddy, I reckon,' Elsdon whispered to his mum.

She went red in the face and slapped his legs real hard.

Mum, Dad and Elsdon left Waiwhetu Road early one morning, before dawn. Elsdon had crept out into the back yard and said goodbye to Snowy. He still wasn't certain that Snowy was there. 'Everyone says cats don't go to Heaven,' Elsdon told the shallow grave. 'I reckon you must be there, they've prob'ly told a fib.'

The car trailer was piled high with boxes and furniture. They had sold the rest. Mrs Daniels was bawling into her apron. She'd hugged Elsdon so hard he felt sick from the onion smell. Auntie Vida and Uncle Bill had sent Elsdon a book of stories with pictures about a little boy who was brought up by animals. Elsdon clutched the book tightly, sitting on the back seat of the car. Of Uncle Bryce nothing was said. He hadn't been to see them, hadn't sent a note. Elsdon asked his mum where he was and she went funny, all white and pasty looking. She and his dad looked at each other for a long time but didn't answer him. His mum hugged him. 'We love you, Elsdon' was all she said.

The car was a Morris Minor and seemed real posh to Elsdon even if the insides were all ripped and it was second-hand. They had never owned a car before. Even Mrs Rahana came out on to the road to wave tata. Mrs Daniels thrust a bag of liquorice lollies through the car window. The bag broke and the lollies fell to the floor. His mum had bought a new hat with feathers in it. Wendy Daniels watched them from the front porch of the house. Elsdon thought she looked like a dead person. He knew what a dead person looked like.

Elsdon didn't say tata to anyone except Snowy and Mrs Nation, who weren't there anyway. He felt a bit crook, but didn't tell his mum. Going to the Waikato seemed like going to the other side of the world. 'They'll be a bit cow-cocky up there, I reckon,' he told himself, having heard his dad say that earlier to his mum.

6 The House down Canada Street

Elsdon was looking through the small window of his room. On the other side of the hedge was a truck full of cattle. He didn't know if they were cows or bulls and wasn't really sure what the difference between them was. The cattle were keeping him awake, all mooing and moaning.

'Making a racket like that,' he said, his face pressed to the glass, 'a bloke wouldn't credit it. I s'pose you miss being in the paddock.'

He had watched two blokes herding the cattle from the paddock into the truck just after tea. He knew they'd stay outside his window on the shunting-tracks until the next morning. The track ran along beside their hedge and was used night and day. Elsdon hated the noise. He hated being in Morrinsville too. He, Dad and Mum had been there for a month. Their house was right next door to the railway-yard. On the other side of the house was the Holeproof swimsuit factory where his dad was the manager. There were no other houses in the street, it was full of factories. He missed Waiwhetu Road so much he had cried every night for a week. Now he had to go to school every day and they went to the Gospel Hall at least two times a week. The other blokes at school were always slinging off at him because he was a dunce and a townie and a holy roller. For his birthday he had been given a leather-bound Bible, a new *Radio Fun* annual and a wind-up tin toy which had already been broken. Elsdon was ten. The changes in his life had begun.

Morrinsville was almost right in the middle of the Wai-kato cow country, a rich farming area in New Zealand. The town was surrounded by farms and twenty miles away from Hamilton, the nearest city. There was a main street, Thames Street, two picture-houses called the Regent and the Deluxe, a public swimming-pool in which you could catch live frogs, and because his dad was manager of a fac-tory the blokes in his class thought his mum and dad were rolling in money. Elsdon thought it all pretty queer. He'd begun to talk to Jesus, who was his only friend apart from Maurice, who lived along the rail-track.

'I'd be better off pushing up the daisies, Jesus,' Elsdon had begun to say whenever he was on his own down the back of the section. He didn't talk to Jesus in front of Mum. She would give him a hiding for no reason at all these days. Most days Elsdon felt real fed up. He seemed to be on his own now more than he'd ever been in Waiwhetu Road. There were no neighbours and he wasn't allowed to talk to the women who worked in the factory. A lot of them were Maoris and his mum told him they were heathen. His dad was trying to get them to go to the Gospel Hall so they could be saved, born again in Jesus.

Sometimes he would sit on the concrete which ran along the front of the house with his lizard. He had found the lizard down the back and kept it in a box filled with clods of earth. Elsdon hoped the women might notice him. The cafeteria windows faced the side of the house and the women had their lunch at the tables beside the windows. Elsdon would take the lizard out of its box and try to feed it with matchsticks he had dipped in honey. No one told him what food to give the lizard and he tried all sorts of grub he took from the kitchen safe.

'You're not to fritter away food, Elsdon,' his mum kept telling him. 'We can't afford it.'

Elsdon's mum was moaning quite a bit now. She never

had any time for him and spent hours every day in the wash-house or in the back yard tending the veges. When he got home from school she would pour him a glass of milk from the billy, leave him two bran biscuits and go back to what she'd been doing.

Tea was always at five o'clock, when Dad walked over from the factory. Elsdon might walk down the rail-tracks to see his friend Maurice, or cross the road and stare at the bulls in the paddock. His dad had said they were bulls. They would stare back and Elsdon would talk to them.

'If Mrs Daniels was here, she could let her chooks run around with you bulls,' he would say. 'I reckon you've got enough room. Have you ever been to Wellington? It's better than here. We've got lots more room here though and my dad's a manager now. I've got a friend called Maurice, he lives down the rail-tracks. I had a cat in Wellington called Snowy and he got runned over, my dad found him. But he might have been eaten by a Chinaman.'

Elsdon would offer the bulls clumps of grass he pulled up from the verge. The bulls seemed eager to eat it even though they had lots of grass in the paddock.

Elsdon, his mum and dad had taken nearly a week to travel up from Wellington in the second-hand Morris Minor. The car had broken down numerous times. Once the trailer had become detached and had rolled into a ditch, spilling all the boxes and breaking some of Mum's crockery.

Their first stop overnight had been with Uncle Judah and Aunt Una at Masterton. It was the only time during the trip that Elsdon slept in a real bed. The rest of the nights he slept on the back seat of the car. His mum and dad slept in a tent they erected on the roadside.

Aunt Una had a mole on her chin with a long hair poking out, which was the first thing Elsdon noticed about her. He had not seen it since he'd been a baby, so of course didn't remember it. Aunt Una didn't wear lipstick like his mum sometimes did, and Elsdon heard her say that wearing stockings was worldly, like lipstick. His mum stopped wearing either after that. She acted a bit scared of Aunt Una, who would tweak Elsdon's cheeks every moment she could and ask him questions about what he might like to be once he had grown up. She thought he should plan to be a missionary and travel to India with the Lord's message. Uncle Judah didn't have much to say to Elsdon. He read the Bible to them for almost an hour before they were allowed to eat. When he'd finished reading, he asked Elsdon to say grace.

Elsdon didn't know what he was supposed to say. They all stared at him in silence, so he muttered, 'Two, four, six, eight, bog in don't wait', which he had heard at school.

His mum cried out and slapped him across the legs. When tea was finished he was sent straight to bed.

There were no books in the house except the Bible, no radio, and the only picture on any of the walls was Holman Hunt's painting of Jesus knocking on the door. Elsdon had stared at it for a long time, then asked his mum if Jesus really looked like that. His mum looked daggers at him, then seemed a bit embarrassed but didn't hit him.

There was a son called Aubrey, who painted watercolours of beaches and trees. When he talked his hands flew about all over the place. Aunt Una called him her little artistic sunbeam. To Elsdon, cousin Aubrey looked as old as Uncle Bryce, but not as friendly. He heard his mum telling his dad, 'He might be artistic, Len, but I think he's a bit of a drip.'

Elsdon lay in his bed clutching his book of stories about the little boy who'd been brought up by animals. He stared at the ceiling waiting for his mum to come and tuck him in. She didn't come. He fell asleep with the light on.

The following morning they left early after breakfast. Elsdon didn't see Uncle Judah or Aubrey who were still asleep. Aunt Una gave him a kiss on the forehead and the hair on her chin tickled his nose and made him sneeze snot all over the front of her dress.

'I'm ashamed of you, Elsdon,' his mum said after they were on their way. 'If we weren't leaving this morning, you would have had a real good hiding.' His dad didn't say anything.

Elsdon sat quietly on the back seat of the car and stared out at the passing land. 'Enough to make a bloke sick,' he whispered to himself.

The best part of the journey was when they stayed in a camp just outside Rotorua. Elsdon had to sleep in the car of course but it all seemed different. There were lots of other people he could watch, except his mum wouldn't let him wander off and he didn't speak to anyone, as she told him that they would all be heathen. The morning after they arrived they took him along to see the mud-pools and the geysers and where the Maoris cooked their food under the ground. There was steam rising everywhere Elsdon looked and it was real scary. He'd liked to have stomped about in the mud-pools in his gumboots. He had a glass of mineral water and an ice-block.

On the way out, after they'd stood on the bridge throwing pennies into the water for the Maori kiddies, his mum told him, 'We can't stay any longer, Elsdon, we've a long road ahead', and he put his foot in a cooking-hole accidentally and scorched his leg. He didn't yell or anything and felt very brave.

'You should watch where you're walking, Elsdon! Where's your gumption?' his mum said. She rubbed a sticky ointment over his leg when they got back to the campsite.

That night he hadn't been able to sleep. He tried to talk to Jesus. 'I'm not very happy, I reckon,' he said, staring through the car window at the sky. 'I heard Mum saying that I'm not the full quid, but I don't suppose you mind, Jesus. I didn't want to leave Waiwhetu Road. It isn't my fault that my dad got the boot and we're having to go and live in the sticks. It isn't right, Jesus.'

There was no sign that Jesus had heard him. There was still a light on in the tent so he pulled on his dressing-gown, opened the door of the car and walked across the grass. He stood near the tent entrance and squatted down, his hands resting on his knees. Elsdon listened.

As usual his mum was yacking away and he thought his dad might be asleep.

'I don't know how we'll be able to pay Bill back that loan,' Elsdon's mum was saying. 'You won't be getting much money. I suppose I'll have to go out and get work too.'

'No you won't,' his dad mumbled. 'I want you at home, where you're meant to be. It isn't right for a man's wife to be working. It's heathen.'

They were silent for a while. Elsdon put his head closer to the canvas. He could hear rustling sounds.

'I don't know what we will have to face with Elsdon,' his mum started off again. 'He seems to be getting worse. It doesn't come from my side of the family, it must be yours. None of my side of the family are like him. It worries me sick. Mrs Daniels was always asking me odd questions about him. She could see he isn't the full quid. It'll get worse, mind you, it'll get worse as he grows older. We should never have had him. Sometimes I think we're being punished.'

50

'For what?' his dad muttered.

'Backsliding. We're backsliders, you and me. It's made me so confused. I blame you, of course, and your family. My family have done quite well without the Brethren. Sometimes I wonder if. . . .' And she fell silent.

'You mustn't talk that way, Jessie,' his dad said, loudly. 'There's only one path for us, the narrow one. Your family are sinners and you should be thankful that through me you have found the Lord. We're about to make a fresh start, with His help.'

Elsdon's mum was silent until he heard her bawling her eyes out. He hurried back to the car, curling up on the back seat. In the darkness he rocked back and forth, holding his knees tightly against his chest.

The following morning he had forgotten all about what he'd heard and reckoned that he'd had a bad dream. All the way along the road they took he thought about the geysers he had seen and the Maori cooking-holes and the little Maori kiddies in the nuddy diving for pennies, which they stored in their mouths. He kept examining his scorched leg so much his mum gave him a telling-off, while his dad cleared his throat again and again as if he had a frog in it.

He sat quietly after that on the back seat of the Morris Minor. He thought about what it might be like living in the Waikato. He'd been told about the Waikato at school when they heard he was being taken there. It was full of cows and acres of farms and there were no tall buildings like there were in Wellington. He thought it might be better now his dad was going to be a manager of a factory. Yet inside him there appeared a still, small voice telling him over and over again that somewhere up ahead something crook might happen and there would not be anything he could do about it. Although he thought his mum had been going to die and she hadn't. He'd thought that Snowy had been eaten by a Chinaman and that wasn't true, his dad reckoned. In his mind though, there were big shadowy things like bogy men and he feared that one day the bogy men might come out and give them all a bit of a fright.

Elsdon didn't really mind the new school in Morrinsville. For a while his teacher was very interested in him and had no worries when he butted in to ask questions. The others left him alone most of the time, but he was pretty sure they didn't like him. The names he was called behind his back were no worse than the names he'd been called at the school in Waiwhetu Road. He enjoyed nature study most of all because then they would go down to the stream and he was able to sit beside his teacher on the grass. She would tell him things about pukekos and how the Maori people made baskets from flax. Elsdon told his teacher that his mum thought all Maoris were heathen and not the Lord's children, and his teacher frowned, then hugged him.

The following day she sent a note home with Elsdon and when his mum had read it she really did her block and gave him a hiding. Elsdon wasn't told why. His mum sent a long letter back to the headmaster, and after that Elsdon's teacher didn't seem as nice. 'No worries,' Elsdon told himself.

He had begun to like being at school because life with Mum and Dad wasn't any good now. They were always having rows. Elsdon would listen to them rowing until they realized he was there. Then they would hurry off into the bathroom and lock the door and carry on, thinking that Elsdon couldn't hear. He would sit on the floor outside the bathroom with his ear against the wood. His body would shake a bit as he listened. He learned a lot but didn't understand what all of it meant. The things he did understand caused a closing-in of the world around him, made him know what being lonely meant. He would wander off down the section to sit in the long grass and talk to Jesus.

'I've been getting to know a lot lately, Jesus. It was Mrs Daniels who got Mrs Nation taken away. I heard my mum telling Dad that. Mum had a letter. I thought Mrs Daniels was my friend, but she couldn't be if she had Mrs Nation took to the mental house. She didn't even ask how I was in the letter. Mum didn't tell me about it, I listened to them yacking in the kitchen and through the bathroom door. Uncle Bryce's been put into a hospital at Porirua, where bad people who aren't all there are put. I think that's where Mrs Nation is too. Uncle Bryce isn't mental, I know he isn't. It's enough to make a bloke sick. Mum told Dad that he did dirty things with other blokes and that was a sin which'd send him all the way to Hell, even if he was her brother.'

Elsdon felt that his talking to Jesus stopped him from bawling his eyes out too much, which his dad said was sissy. Elsdon didn't really mind. The talking helped, though. He wished Jesus would talk back to him and began to wonder if He was really up there living in the sky. It seemed a heck of a funny place to live. He had asked his teacher if she had seen Jesus, or knew Him like his mum and dad said they did. His teacher had looked sad and Elsdon thought she might cry. 'I'm sorry, little man,' she had said. 'I'm not to talk to you about that. I've been warned.'

He didn't ask her again. Most days now, since she had been to see the headmaster, she would not smile at him in class like she used to. She wouldn't let him butt in and ask questions. When he put his hand up she looked the other way. The others in the class would giggle. His teacher would look real crook. Elsdon didn't understand why. He began to feel he wasn't there, but at least being in the class-room was still better than being at home listening to Mum and Dad in a paddy with each other and giving him hidings whenever they felt like it.

He tried to ask Maurice about Jesus one day while they were sitting in the bush beside the stream. The surface of the water was covered with milk curds from the big factory where milk was put into bottles. Maurice had been throw-ing rocks into the curds and swearing. Elsdon had learned a lot of new words but had promised Maurice never to repeat them in front of his mum and dad.

'Jesus is only up there to punish us,' Maurice told Elsdon.

They had got to know one another through having to go to the Gospel Hall. Maurice had stared at Elsdon a lot during the meetings, then grinned every time he saw him. Elsdon had seen Maurice at school and would share his vegemite sandwiches behind the bike sheds.

'You can be my mate if you like,' Maurice had sugges-ted. 'You're not a dunce, I reckon. The other blokes, they don't like anyone new. You'll have no worries now we're mates.'

Secretly Elsdon began to look up to Maurice like he'd looked up to Uncle Bryce. He thought the two were alike, but didn't say so, even to Jesus. He reckoned that Maurice was his best friend and it made him warm inside. Yet what Maurice said when they were on their own sometimes made him nervy.

'One of these days I shall bugger off out of it,' he'd tell Elsdon. 'I'll go up north to Auckland and get a bloody job, save up money and go to England, where the poms are. The poms are pretty good, I reckon. My grandad was one of them and he was real beaut. None of this Brethren lark for him. He was a boozer and loved the trots, went every Saturday.'

Maurice laughed like a loony when Elsdon said it seemed pretty funny his grandad liking to have a poo only on Saturday. When he stopped laughing he gave Elsdon a quick, rough hug. 'The trots is horses, Els, not having a poo. It's the races. You put bets on horses pulling carts with big wheels and a bloke driving called a jockey and you win money. Or you lose it. One day when we're grown up I'll take you there.'

Sometimes when they mucked about down by the stream Maurice would have a real gloomy face and Elsdon would feel a bit nervy of him. Maurice was big and strong but he said he would always be Elsdon's mate, whatever happened.

'Perhaps we'll bugger off to England together, mate, one of these days. I'll take care of you and we'll go to the trots and drink beer and have real beaut times with the poms.'

Elsdon would look up at Maurice's face and grin with pleasure.

'I hate those bastards at the Hall,' Maurice would say on his black days. 'My dad gives most of his money to the buggers and we're always broke in our family. The bastards even want to start a special school so none of us Brethren kids will have to go to a proper one. But I don't reckon the Government will allow it. Anyway, I'd stop my little brother and sister going, I reckon, that's for bloody sure.'

Maurice's brother and sister were both younger than Elsdon and went to the primary school. Elsdon and Maurice went to the intermediate.

'Not even allowed to go to the pictures on Saturdays like all the other kids do. Bloody stinkers. Have you ever been to the picture-house, Els?'

Elsdon shook his head. He wasn't really very sure what the pictures were. He had stood outside the Regent sometimes and it all looked pretty exciting. Maurice explained.

Elsdon said one of the swear-words, then giggled and reckoned that when he was big he'd go every Saturday and in the week as well instead of to prayer meetings.

'We could go together, mate,' Maurice said.

'Is Jesus a real man?' Elsdon asked his friend. 'Why can't we see Him? Doesn't He ever come down from the sky? Mum said I'm not allowed to say His name until I get saved. Then she says I won't get saved. I talk to Jesus a lot and I reckon He tries to listen. He never talks back, though. Are you saved, Maurice?'

'There's no such thing as getting saved,' Maurice told him. 'It's all a load of stinking bull. I shan't get saved, not by the Brethren, and I'll stop my brother and sister too.'

Maurice had a ·303 rifle, of which he was very proud. His mum and dad didn't seem to mind his having it, in fact he had been given it for his fourteenth birthday. 'Dad said it would make me into a real man,' Maurice told Elsdon.

He would use the rifle in the bush, shooting at Coca Cola bottles propped up on fallen tree trunks. He showed Elsdon how to use it, squatting down behind him with his arms about Elsdon, steadying the barrel. With a great deal of help Elsdon shot two Coca Cola bottles and a raspberry jam tin. He felt pretty proud and Maurice said he was the best mate a bloke could wish for.

Elsdon asked his mum if he could have a rifle, and was given a severe beating with the razor-strop. He wasn't supposed to be friendly with Maurice even though his mum and dad were leading lights at the Gospel Hall.

'He's far too old for you, Elsdon,' his mum had told him several times. 'You need a friend your own age. Maurice will only lead you astray. He's a wild boy, that one. He's not a good influence. He's a sinner, Elsdon. He's never been saved.'

Elsdon didn't reckon Maurice was a sinner. Maurice was his friend. He thought his mum didn't want him to have a friend, but didn't tell her that. 'It's enough to make a bloke sick, Jesus,' he would say. 'All my mum does now is moan and grumble and tell me off and give me hidings. It isn't right.'

Maurice had an anger that often made Elsdon feel jittery. Maurice hated the Brethren so much that Elsdon could not help but be influenced by the hate. Slowly as time went by it began to show itself in things he said in front of his mum and dad. Very soon he suffered more and more hidings, and was locked in his room for hours.

He reckoned his mum didn't like him any more. His dad was always over at the factory. Sometimes he wouldn't come home until after Elsdon had been sent to bed. At the Sunday morning meetings his dad was always quoting things from the Bible and talking about sin and redemption. It seemed to Elsdon that he was on his feet in the Hall more than anyone else. At mealtimes he would read to them from the Bible, as Uncle Judah had done when they stayed in Masterton. Elsdon heard a still, small voice inside him. It comforted him, he felt as though he wasn't so alone.

Days went by without Elsdon's seeing Maurice. Maurice would never come to the house down Canada Street. Elsdon was quite welcome at Maurice's. At least no one moaned or told him off when he was there. Maurice's dad once asked if he was saved. When Elsdon said no he wasn't, he was told he would be prayed for every night. After his dad had said that, Maurice looked as if he were about to explode. His body shook and his face went scarlet and he'd rushed out the back door shouting something.

One day Elsdon was given an apple and a pear from their orchard, which he took home. His mum said nothing, took the fruit off him and threw it in the bin.

She had grown very silent when they were alone together. Elsdon would watch her talking to herself while she was hanging out the daily wash. Sometimes she would stop what she was doing and stare up at the sky, threatening it with her fist and shouting out words Elsdon couldn't hear. He would stay away from his mum when she was like that. It was more scary when he saw her staring at him. He would be sitting at the kitchen table playing with the Meccano or trying to do his homework and he would feel her watching. He had looked up only the one time. Her face and the look in her eyes had made him feel real nervy, deep down inside. 'Mum's getting to be a bit of a loony, I reckon,' he would tell himself when she was out of earshot.

He hardly saw his dad. The factory became his dad's real home. Elsdon had heard his mum shouting that late one night. The only times when Elsdon knew he would see his dad were on Wednesday nights for the prayer meetings and on Sundays. They would ride to the Gospel Hall in the car, Elsdon sitting on the back seat and his mum and dad in front not saying a word.

Elsdon would try to talk to them. 'Looks like it might bucket down tonight,' he would say loudly. Or, 'This car's real comfy, isn't it, Mum. I bet the bulls in the paddock would like to get in here. They look worn out.'

Sometimes he would tell them about school, not stopping until his dad had parked the car outside the Hall. Often his mum would turn her head and glare at him when he talked. Other nights when they drove to the Hall Elsdon would remain silent. He would listen to the still, small voice inside his head, and find comfort there.

Auntie Vida, and Maurice's little brother and sister, were killed within days of each other. Elsdon heard the news through his habit of listening to his mum and dad talking in the kitchen after he'd been sent to bed. Creeping out into the hall, crouching low on the floor in the dark.

Auntie Vida and Uncle Bill had been in their car and it had crashed off the road into a gully. They had been travelling up to visit. The car had overturned. Acid from the battery had dripped all over Auntie Vida's face after she'd been killed. Uncle Bill had a broken leg and was badly shocked and bruised. He was in a hospital. There had been a cable sent to Canada Street and Auntie Vida had been dead for a whole night before she and Uncle Bill were found. Elsdon's dad had telephoned the hospital from the factory. When they'd been found, Uncle Bill was holding Auntie Vida in his arms and wouldn't let her go.

Elsdon began to tremble, sitting there in the dark. The bogy men were coming out. He was too scared to go back to his room, too scared to go to his mum and dad for comfort. They had known about the accident for days.

'It's a judgement,' his mum kept saying. 'It's judgement for our backsliding. I can't go on!'

Elsdon's dad didn't say anything, while his mum kept saying 'It's a judgement, Len' as they sat there in the kitchen.

Elsdon was still crouched on the hall floor when the banging came on the back door, along with the sound of a wailing voice. Elsdon heard his dad unlocking the door and crawled to the end of the hall so he could peer round the corner. It was one of the women from the Gospel Hall, and her husband. The woman had her white pinny pulled up, covering her face, her body rocking back and forth as if she were about to fall down. Her husband stood looking grim and white-faced with what Elsdon thought to be anger. When the woman let the apron fall her face was white too, as white as the pinny. Her mouth was dribbling. Elsdon would have heard her from his room she was wailing the words so loudly.

Maurice, Elsdon's best friend apart from Jesus, had been at home looking after his little brother and sister while his mum and dad were at an extra prayer meeting at the Hall. Maurice had loaded his ·303 rifle, gone into the back bedroom where the little tykes were asleep, and shot both of them in the head.

7   A Meeting in the Paddock

Auntie Vida had left Elsdon a large sum of money in her will.

'It's to be put in a trust for you, Elsdon,' his mum told him. 'It'll be kept safe until you are twenty-one.'

Elsdon's mum hadn't explained what a trust was, and he didn't ask. She was acting a bit crook almost all the time now, in Elsdon's opinion. She had started to sing hymns very loudly while she was in the wash-house and would often tell him, 'We are all wicked sinners, Elsdon.' And, 'You must ask the Lord every night for help to be born again. I'm sick with worry.'

She would stare at him a lot. Some nights he would wake up in bed and get a real fright when he saw her sitting in a chair on the far side of his bedroom. She would be holding a Bible and rocking backward and forward, and muttering. One night he opened his eyes and she was holding her wooden rolling-pin over his head and he cried out and she ran from the room. Elsdon would close his eyes tight and pretend he hadn't woken up at all.

'It's enough to make a bloke go and get shickered,' he told the bulls in the paddock across the road. 'I get lots of hidings now. I got one yesterday and Mum said it would stop me from being a sinner. I don't think I'm a sinner, I reckon. Look at that,' he said, lifting up his leg and showing the bulls where it was bruised.

His teacher at school asked him where the bruises came from.

'Oh, no worries,' Elsdon told her. 'I felled over.'

'Fell over, Elsdon,' his teacher corrected him. She stared at him for a long time, with a frown on her face. 'How are things at home, little man?' she asked.

'All right, I reckon,' Elsdon said, not looking at her. 'Dad said we might have some chooks in the back yard. He'll build a house for them and I'd be able to look after one. We had some chooks in Wellington but they really belonged to Mrs Daniels and Mum helped herself to the eggs.'

His teacher had sent two more notes to his mum. They had been ripped up and flushed down the lavatory too. Elsdon's mum didn't say anything about the notes. The same night she came into his bedroom with the razor-strop and gave him a hiding.

'My bum's real sore,' Elsdon told her in the morning. There had been blood on the sheets when he woke up.

'If you're not good I'll knock you into the middle of next week!' his mum shouted.

Elsdon's dad said nothing at all and just kept clearing his throat and making coughing noises. Elsdon felt more and more that he wasn't there, when his dad looked at him. His dad hardly ever talked to him. He wouldn't let Elsdon visit the factory.

'It's full of heathen women, it isn't nice', he was told, when he asked his mum.

'If he doesn't like those heaving women,' Elsdon said aloud to himself later, 'he shouldn't work there.'

Elsdon wished he'd been able to tell Maurice about the money he was going to get. Instead he told the bulls in the paddock. He didn't think it was right to tell Jesus. They were always going on at the Gospel Hall that Jesus thought money was the root of all evil. Elsdon wasn't sure now if Jesus really could be his friend. 'I'm getting a lot of money,' he told the bulls. 'It's going to be put in a truss until I get old. I don't know what a truss is but it'll keep my money safe. Mum said.'

The bulls stared back with huge brown eyes.

Elsdon gave them some clumps of grass to eat.

He was never to see Maurice again.

He had heard lots of people yacking about the murders, on his way to school. People would gather outside their houses and yack away about anything, but during the weeks that followed the news Elsdon saw and heard a lot more people than usual. The others at school had known Maurice was Elsdon's friend and many of them, some children of the Brethren, began to avoid Elsdon or say nasty things behind his back, worse than before.

A photograph of Maurice was printed beside an article on the front page of the local newspaper, with a headline saying *Gospel Killing*. Elsdon tried to read all the words, but it had been easier listening to people in the street.

'He said he didn't want them to be dragged up with the rest of the Brethren as he had' he'd heard one lady tell another.

'Wicked, wicked, he must have been touched,' the other lady uttered.

'Oh, those poor little tykes. Something should be done, Dorothea, something should be done. They're a nasty lot, those Brethren, altogether. You mark my words!'

Elsdon walked across to where the ladies stood and stared up into their faces. 'I'm a bit shook. I was Maurice's best friend. We could've gone to the pictures. It isn't right.'

Both women went red in the face and hurried off.

Red paint was tipped on the steps outside the Gospel Hall. One of the Brethren was attacked in the street and given a bloody nose. On a side wall of the Hall someone wrote in white paint *All Holy Rollers Should Be Shot*. Very few seemed to lay the blame on Maurice. They pitied him. The Brethren were not liked much in Morrinsville.

Maurice had been taken away and Elsdon heard he'd been put into a place called Borstal. He learned at school that Borstal was like a prison for kiddies. For a while his mum would not say a thing to Elsdon about what had happened. She and Dad had caught him listening the night the lady brought the news. His dad had pulled Elsdon up from the floor and carried him off to his room, locking him in, and he stayed there until late the next morning. Elsdon had been so upset he'd gone to the toilet in his pyjamas and wet the bed twice during the long, long night. For that he was given a hiding and wasn't allowed to go to school the next day. He sat on the spring base of his bed and held his book of stories. The mattress his mum had to wash and hang over the clothes-line in the back yard.

There had been a lot of comings and goings that morning. People from the Gospel Hall held a prayer meeting with his mum while his dad was at work over in the factory. When his mum went off to the shops Elsdon left his room after finding the door unlocked. He turned on the radio and sat on the floor in front of it. He wanted to listen and talk to Aunt Daisy. 'They took my friend away,' he told her. 'They took Mrs Nation away like that, but she and Maurice aren't in the same place. Maurice done in his brother and sister 'cause he didn't want them to be Brethrens. He's gone to a place called Borstal. That's a prison.'

Elsdon knew Aunt Daisy couldn't hear him, but pretending she was there made him feel a bit better. He was telling her more about what had gone on when his mum arrived back, rushed into the room and turned the radio off. 'You're a wicked boy!' she shouted at him. 'It's that Maurice, he's poisoned your mind. I don't know what your dad will have to say about this', and she belted Elsdon across the head with the back of her hand.

Elsdon didn't cry, he was very brave.

'A bloke wouldn't credit it,' he told Jesus when he was back in his room. 'I dunno why Mum's in a paddy with me. I didn't do anything.'

The following Sunday Maurice's dad stood up in front of the Brethren at the morning meeting and yacked away for an hour. The only thing that Elsdon remembered him saying was that Maurice had been poisoned by Satan and that he was mad.

Elsdon didn't think his friend could be mad. 'If he'd been mad, Jesus,' he said as he lay in bed that night, 'blokes in white coats might've taken him away, like they took Mrs Nation, I reckon. They said she was mad. But I heard them say it was some coppers took him, in a car.'

Elsdon was told he must come straight home after school and not linger, not to talk to anyone he might meet on the way. 'That boy's tainted you, Elsdon,' his mum told him. 'I'm not sure any more if you can be saved. That Maurice has put poison in you against the Lord and we will have to punish you a great deal before the Lord will forgive.'

Forced as he was to do without Maurice, uncertain that Jesus could be his friend when his mum gave him hidings on His behalf – 'The Lord's so angry at you!' his mum would yell as she beat his legs and bottom with the razor-strop – Elsdon found his world a confused, lonely place. No wonder he dawdled all the way home from school, stopped to stare in shop windows and stood outside the Regent picture-house, staring at the display photographs.

One afternoon he wandered into the Dairy Milk Bar which was on the corner of Canada Street. He stood in front of the long counter and stared at the pictures stuck all over the walls. He wasn't given pocket-money like the other boys in his class so he couldn't buy anything. He was given sandwiches for lunch, wrapped in greaseproof paper inside a tin which his mum washed out every night with carbolic soap so that it stank.

'What can I do for you, mate?' boomed a voice from behind the counter.

'I'm only looking, I reckon,' Elsdon said to the big man.

The man had a red face and was acting pretty friendly, in Elsdon's opinion.

'Do you get your milk from bulls?' Elsdon asked. 'We've got bulls in the paddock over the road and I go and talk to them and they listen. They're real interesting, I reckon. I'm not supposed to come in here, as Mum said it's sinful, but I'm getting real fed up not doing what I want. We're getting some chooks soon. My dad's going to build a hen-house and I'll have a chook to look after. I like the smells in here and I don't reckon it's sinful. The other day I . . .'

'Whoa, whoa, hang on a bit!' The big man was laughing and Elsdon grinned. 'You're going on like a bull at a gate. What's your name, son?'

'Elsdon Bird,' said Elsdon.

'Oh yeah, your dad runs the Holeproof factory. I know,' the big man said.

'We belong to the Brethrens,' Elsdon told him.

The big man moved off, smiling now but looking sad at the same time. He produced a huge Hokey Pokey ice-cream. Elsdon had never seen one so huge before. The man handed it to him then came out from behind the counter and put his arm around Elsdon's shoulders. 'You're a bit of a beaut,' he said. 'You have a good go at the ice-cream. Enjoy it, Elsdon. And don't you worry a flaming bugger about anything.'

'I won't, I reckon,' Elsdon said, adding a thank-you and walking off towards the doorway. He wasn't sure if he should have taken the ice-cream and felt a bit bothered.

'You come back and talk to me again!' the big man shouted to Elsdon as he left.

'Poor little blighter,' Elsdon heard him say to someone else inside the Dairy Milk Bar. 'What a blinking shame, a beaut little joker like that amongst those holy rollers. It makes my bloody blood boil.'

Elsdon wandered down Canada Street licking his ice-cream.

'Hokey Pokey's the best in the whole world, I reckon,' he told the bulls when he reached the paddock. They were on the far side beneath cabbage trees and didn't hear him.

When he walked round to the back of the house his mum was coming out from the wash-house. Her face was sweating and her hands were red-raw from scrubbing clothes. 'Where have you been?' she shouted at him. 'I've been worried sick about you!'

She stared at the half-finished ice-cream in Elsdon's hand. Without saying anything more she took the ice-cream away from him and threw it across the hedge. Then she hit Elsdon across the side of the head with her fist. Elsdon was knocked to the ground, lay on the concrete path and began to cry. 'I won't have it, do you hear me!' she shouted.

Uncle Bill was still in hospital being nursed with his broken leg.

'We'll have to get him up here' Elsdon heard his mum telling his dad. They were sitting at the kitchen table and Elsdon was listening from the hall. 'He's nowhere else to go. He can't look after himself when he gets out.'

His dad didn't say anything. Elsdon was too nervy to peer into the room. They thought he was asleep. It was real dark outside and Elsdon thought it must be the middle of the night.

67

'He can sleep in Elsdon's bed,' his mum went on. 'Elsdon can have the camp-bed. Bill can't go back to live in Petone, it's too worrying. I don't know how we'll manage.'

'The Lord will provide, Jess,' Elsdon's dad suddenly said. 'He always has.'

They said nothing for a long while. Elsdon could hear his mum sighing. 'That son of his is coming back for the funeral,' she said quietly. 'We should go down for it, Len. Bill's in a bad way. He's gone a bit crook, the doctor said.'

'We can't if Bill's coming straight here,' Elsdon's dad muttered.

'I didn't think about that. It's the worry, Len, the worry. It's turning my mind. Of course Bill will want to go. She's being buried by the Catholics.'

'He can come up here after, Jessie. I'm not letting you go to a Catholic funeral, Bill or no Bill.'

Elsdon crept back to his room and curled up beneath the blankets in bed. He lay awake and whispered. There were some cows or bulls in a shunter near his window and he whispered to them. 'My uncle's coming up here to live. Auntie Vida got killed in a car. I liked her, she would've been my friend. Uncle Bill has a broked leg. Mum says he's crook. We'll have to look after him a lot, I reckon.'

Elsdon was not told about Auntie Vida, he knew only because he had listened in to his mum and dad. He had learned about Maurice the same way. He didn't understand why they hadn't told him or spoken to him about things. He wasn't a baby.

The Brethren had a funeral for Maurice's little brother and sister a week after they'd died. Elsdon wasn't allowed to go. He was told to stay in his room while his mum and dad were there. 'I'll pray about you at the funeral, Elsdon,' his mum told him.

During the next few weeks Elsdon was shut in his room almost every night. When his dad wasn't there his mum came in with the razor-strop, made him take his pyjama bottom down and whipped him until she was out of breath. She took away his book of stories and made him have his Bible instead. It had no pictures in it and the words were too small for him to read.

Elsdon was told he must learn the Bible. 'It's the only book you'll need in life,' his mum told him. 'Not that other rubbish. I want you to learn that Bible off by heart, do you hear me! You're a sinner, Elsdon. This will be your sal-vation. Your dad and me want you to be saved. It's for your own good.'

Elsdon grieved for his book of stories about the little boy brought up by animals. He didn't like the Bible and didn't know how he was supposed to learn it. 'Did Jesus write it?' he asked.

'You are not to say His name!' his mum yelled. 'I've told you before. You make me sick with worry, do you know that? I've enough on my plate as it is. The Disciples wrote the Bible as the Lord told them to. That's all you need to know.'

His mum hadn't hugged him, nor held him to her bosom like she used to, for a long time. Her eyes when she looked at him made Elsdon feel all scary inside. She was talking to herself and having arguments with someone he could never see, more and more often, but only when she was alone. Elsdon wasn't able to talk to the bulls in the pad-dock any more, as they had been taken away. He couldn't talk to Maurice and wasn't sure about talking to Jesus, so he said things to himself. 'S'pose I'm getting a bit bonkers like Mum,' he said. He asked his mum where the bulls had gone.

'They're to be made into meat, Elsdon. They are the

Lord's beasts and are provided for our food. They're dead now, Elsdon.'

'Are they up in Heaven?'

'Beasts don't have souls,' his mum said. She was at the sink in the kitchen, scrubbing veges for their tea. 'Beasts don't go to Heaven, there's no room anyway.'

The Brethren were planning a revival meeting, to be held in the paddock across the road, which they'd hired. Elsdon heard his dad telling his mum about it. Maurice's dad was going to be the guest speaker. Only Brethren would be allowed to go.

'Bill can look after Elsdon,' his mum said. 'He'll be with us by then.'

After the Morrinsville revival meeting Maurice's dad would be travelling all over the Waikato speaking at other meetings about Maurice being mad and poisoned by Satan. The news was all over the country now, he heard his mum and dad say. It was a real big scandal.

'He's a good Christian man,' said Elsdon's mum about Maurice's dad. 'He'll be rewarded in Heaven. He didn't deserve to have such sin descended on his family.'

They didn't mention Maurice at all.

'Maurice is gone now,' Elsdon said after he was in bed. 'The bulls are gone too, dead like Snowy and Auntie Vida.'

For the school holidays, which were two weeks away, Elsdon was to be sent off to a farm, which was owned by a young Brethren couple called Mr and Mrs Smythe-Brown.

'You'll be there for a week, Elsdon,' his mum eventually told him. 'They have a little baby girl and you'll be helping Mr Smythe-Brown on the farm. They are good people, good Christian people.'

Elsdon learned that it had been Mr Smythe-Brown who had asked to have Elsdon at the farm for the holidays. Elsdon remembered him from Sunday mornings at the Hall. He always stared at Elsdon and made him feel a bit bothered.

His mum didn't say that she would miss him, nor did she ask him if he wanted to go. Elsdon thought it pretty neat that he was going to a real farm. On the way home from school he went into the Dairy Milk Bar to tell the big man. Elsdon's dad was there. He was handing out tracts to people sitting at the tables. The big man was watching him and looking real annoyed. He didn't notice Elsdon.

'It's enough to make a bloke sick,' Elsdon said on his way down Canada Street. He stood leaning against the paddock fence and watched the revival tent being erected.

Uncle Bill arrived by train two nights before the meeting in the paddock. To Elsdon he looked pretty crook, pale and thin. The plaster had been removed from his leg, but he limped and had a walking-stick. When Uncle Bill saw Elsdon he began to make choking noises. He held a hand over his eyes.

'Go to your room' Elsdon was told.

Elsdon sat on the camp-bed in the far corner of the bed-room, where he was to sleep. He held his box of Meccano in his lap and waited for Uncle Bill to come and see him. 'I s'pose he misses Auntie Vida now she's pushing up the daisies,' he told himself. 'I don't know what I'll tell him about the story-book. Mum prob'ly will say I lost it. It isn't right, I reckon.'

Uncle Bill's eyes were all red and puffy when he came through into the bedroom. Elsdon's mum was carrying his suitcase and unpacked it for him. Uncle Bill wouldn't look at Elsdon. When he'd put on his pyjamas he got into bed and lay on his side with his face to the wall.

'You be quiet now, Elsdon, and get into bed as well.

71

Your uncle's crook and if you make any noise you'll get a hiding.'

Elsdon went to bed without having had any tea. Later, when it was dark outside, his mum came in carrying a mug of cocoa. She put it on the floor beside Elsdon, leaned down and gave him a brief hug. Then she stared at him for such a long time Elsdon closed his eyes tightly. Her face scared him. When he opened his eyes she had gone. He sat up and drank the cocoa, staring at Uncle Bill's shape.

'I'm glad you're here, Uncle Bill,' he said. 'A bloke wouldn't credit it. I get lots of hidings now from my mum, and Dad doesn't talk. They've taken the bulls away like they did Maurice and they're having a rival meeting in the paddock. You can be my friend now you're here, I haven't got one. The blokes at school they think I'm a bit of a dunce and say I'm a holy roller. We could drink some booze, I reckon, when Mum and Dad are at the rival meeting. One day we could go to the trots too.'

Uncle Bill didn't answer. He was snoring in his sleep.

'Enough to make a bloke sick, all this carrying on,' Elsdon said loudly.

Uncle Bill didn't talk very much during the next two days. Elsdon heard him tell his mum that he wasn't interested in joining the Brethren. 'It won't bring Vida back,' he said.

'Elsdon's become a backslider' Elsdon heard his mum tell Uncle Bill. 'It's that Maurice's fault. He went to the devil, that boy, and has poisoned Elsdon's mind. I'm worried sick, Bill, worried sick.'

Uncle Bill muttered something Elsdon didn't hear.

When Elsdon came home from school Uncle Bill would be sitting in a chair out the back. Elsdon would take his milk and bran biscuits and sit on the grass beside him. After sitting there for a while in silence he would reach up

72

and take hold of his uncle's hand. Uncle Bill would stare straight ahead.

'No worries,' Elsdon would say. 'It's a bit of all right you being here. We could get a bit shickered, if you like. I have to go to Mr Smythe-Brown's farm soon for my holiday but I s'pose Mum will look after you. She won't give you any hidings. She sings hymns now when she's scrubbing clothes in the wash-house, and Dad's always over at the factory. He gives out tracts to people and Mum told him off because he preaches to all the heaving women in the cafeteria at lunch-time. She said that women like them couldn't be saved and it's no use trying. They'll try to save you while you're here, I reckon.'

When Uncle Bill failed to reply Elsdon added, 'Will you be my friend? I haven't got one now. I had a friend called Maurice but he was taken away. I said it the other night, but you were snoring so I reckon you didn't hear.'

Uncle Bill began to shake and covered his face with his free hand. Elsdon held on to his other hand tightly. 'I love you, Uncle Bill,' he said. 'I don't mind if you cry. I loved Auntie Vida too. She can't help being died. She was a bit of all right.'

On the night of the revival meeting Elsdon's mum decided that he should go, instead of staying in the house being looked after by Uncle Bill. 'He's too crook to take care of Elsdon,' she told his dad.

They had roast mutton for tea, with kumara and veges from the back yard and boiled apple pudding to follow.

'Dad and me are hoping Elsdon might get saved if we take him with us tonight,' his mum told Uncle Bill, as if Elsdon wasn't at the table. 'They're to ask people at the meeting to come forward and be a witness for Jesus, have their sins washed away by the Lord's kindly light.'

Uncle Bill looked at Elsdon and winked. His mum looked stern. Elsdon's dad read from the Bible once tea was finished. They were still sitting at the table and Uncle Bill nodded off to sleep and nearly fell from his chair.

When Elsdon was struggling to pull on his best shorts and slicking down his hair with water from the basin, Uncle Bill knocked on the bathroom door, came in, and shut it behind him. He sat down on the lavatory seat and leaned forward, elbows on knees, his large hands dangling down. He didn't have his walking-stick with him. 'Well, mate,' he said in his deep voice. 'Do you reckon you like living here in the Waikato?'

'Oh, it's all right, Uncle Bill,' Elsdon said. He was feeling a bit bothered. He knew his mum wouldn't like Uncle Bill being in the bathroom with him. Yet he thought it pretty neat that his uncle had come to talk to him. 'We were going to get some chooks down the back yard,' he told his uncle, 'but I heard Mum doing her block about it to Dad so I don't s'pose we'll get any now. Mum's always doing her block and having paddies. It's enough to make a bloke sick.'

'Your mum's got a lot of worry, old mate,' Uncle Bill told him.

'Elsdon!' they heard his mum shouting. 'Get your skates on, there's a good boy, we're going to be late for the meeting!'

Elsdon thought she was a bit cheered up. He didn't know why, and just hoped for the best.

'Mustn't be late for the meeting, eh?' said Uncle Bill, and he winked again.

To Elsdon even Uncle Bill seemed more cheery. 'No worries,' said Elsdon. 'We won't be late, Uncle Bill.'

Everyone was acting a bit better.

Uncle Bill was coming to the meeting as well, even though he wasn't a Brethren.

'A joker wouldn't credit it, I reckon,' Elsdon added as they left the bathroom together.

Elsdon held Uncle Bill's hand as they crossed the road to the paddock. His mum walked beside him, and his dad on the other side of Uncle Bill.

'We're a big fambly now,' Elsdon said, getting excited.

'Family, Elsdon, family,' his mum corrected him.

She was wearing a new mauve dress and a red hat with artificial fruit on top which Dad had said looked far too worldly. From the tent in the paddock which was lit with electric lights came the sound of hymn singing. Elsdon knew the words of the hymn. He began to join in, swinging his uncle's hand. They were walking slowly because of Uncle Bill's mending leg.

'What a friend we have in Jesus!' sang Elsdon. He looked up at all their faces.

Elsdon's mum was staring straight ahead, holding her handbag tightly against her chest. She looked real serious. Elsdon's dad kept coughing. He frequently looked back over his shoulder at the factory.

The Brethren were half-way through singing 'On the Old Rugged Cross' when Elsdon heard the fire-engines. He looked round the tent but no one else was taking any notice. His mum was belting out the hymn so fiercely, her hat was sliding down her head and her face was scarlet. Uncle Bill had gone very quiet. He was looking pretty crook in Elsdon's opinion and kept wiping his eyes and cheeks with a big white hanky. Elsdon's dad was up the front, being an elder. He was there in case anyone wanted to come forward and get saved. Anyone who wanted to get saved had to walk up the aisle to the front and stand there. Maurice's dad was behind the pulpit. Everyone was sitting on wooden planks propped up by apple-boxes and Elsdon's bum was sore. His mum was staring at him and he knew she was waiting for him to get up and go to the front to get saved.

'I'm not a sinner, I reckon,' Elsdon said aloud, emboldened by all the people around them. 'I'm not going to get saved. It's enough to make a joker sick.'

His mum looked daggers at him. Elsdon sneaked a look at Uncle Bill and felt a bit bothered. He knew he'd get a hiding for saying what he'd said when they got home.

Outside the tent a wind had sprung up. It shook the canvas.

When the fire-engine sirens came closer Elsdon stood up and looked over the heads of the people behind.

'Elsdon, sit down!' his mum hissed. She leaned over to slap him across the legs but missed and nearly fell off the plank. Others began craning their necks and the singing began to falter as the sirens grew louder.

'Crikey!' Elsdon said loudly. 'Something's being burned!' Several people were now rising to their feet. The singing stopped completely, drowned by the noises outside.

In the sudden movement of people beginning to head towards the back of the tent Elsdon lost sight of his mum and Uncle Bill. He found himself being pushed away from them. He could smell smoke now. He saw a way out and crawled underneath the gap in the canvas. There was a great deal of shouting. Figures were hurrying across the grass. Two fire-engines and several cars with headlights glaring were blocking the road.

The Holeproof factory was on fire. The whole building was ablaze, flames roaring up into the black night sky. There was so much smoke Elsdon couldn't see the front of their house. He ran across the paddock to the fence and climbed over. People were crushed in the gateway and a woman had fallen down and was yelling that her leg was hurt.

Elsdon stood in the middle of the road and stared, his

mouth wide open. All round him men were rushing to and fro. He could hear cows and bulls bellowing from a shunter in the railway-yard, and some geezer was yelling out at the top of his voice, 'Get the frigging buckets, you blokes, get the frigging buckets!'

A woman was shrieking. Elsdon could feel the heat on his face. He began to run across the road towards the house. When he was nearly there he fell and grazed his knees on the gravel. He didn't cry, he was very brave. Elsdon scrambled to his feet and hurried forward. 'I'll get our buckets!' he shouted, disappearing into the smoke.

8 In the Wash-house

The fire in the factory destroyed it totally. The coppers were treating it as arson. Someone who hated the Brethren, it was thought. Since Maurice had murdered his little brother and sister, Elsdon's dad had been preaching to the staff every lunch-hour, handing out tracts to shops in Thames Street. Elsdon heard him tell his mum that he didn't think anyone had minded. 'They read the tracts. I've never had trouble. I thought the women enjoyed my little talks.' He sat at the table in the kitchen, his head in his hands. Through the open windows wafted the stink from the fire. The factory was a black, smouldering shambles.

Uncle Bill was out the back in the wash-house, rolling a smoke. He wasn't allowed to smoke inside the house any more. 'It's sinful, Bill,' Elsdon's mum had told him. 'We don't mind you not being interested in the Lord, but you aren't bringing your heathen ways into our home.'

Elsdon had gone out there to see him. 'It'd be neat if I could lick the paper,' Elsdon said, pointing to his uncle's smoke. 'Uncle Bryce used to let me.'

Uncle Bill had his back to the door. He was sitting on a rickety old chair he'd brought in from the shed and still wore his pyjamas. He hadn't shaved for days. When he didn't say anything Elsdon added, 'You can look at my bandages if you like, Uncle Bill.'

Elsdon had burnt his hands in the factory fire. He had run into the house and collected the tin bucket from below the kitchen sink, filling it with water from the outside tap.

In the general chaos no one had seen him struggling towards the blaze. A fireman had found him lying on the grass, a burning plank of wood angled across his arms. Elsdon had been overcome by the smoke. 'I was real brave, I reckon,' he said to himself later.

Few treated him that way. Even the fireman had been angry. A doctor had been rushed to the house to treat Elsdon's burns. 'You're a bit of a scallywag,' he'd told Elsdon, giving him a wink.

'I felled over,' Elsdon explained. 'Nearly busted my boiler. I was trying to put the blinking fire out.'

Elsdon had been given something to make him sleep and been tucked up in his old bed. Uncle Bill spent that night on the camp-bed.

Kept home from school, Elsdon was there when the coppers came to ask his dad questions. 'Some bloke rang the station,' he heard one of the coppers say. 'Said the fire was deliberate. Claimed that you kept asking the women to get born again, join your sect. Said a lot else too. Can't tell you in front of your lady wife. You'll have to come down to the station.'

Elsdon's dad went off in the police car. Elsdon watched from the front veranda.

'We are being punished by the Lord,' his mum said. 'We were backsliders for too long and the Lord is angered.'

She began to bang pots and pans about in the kitchen, after the coppers and Dad had gone. Then she rushed out into the back yard. She glared up at the sky and shook her fist and shouted, 'Leave us alone! I'm at the end of my tether!'

From the ruins of the factory where firemen were still going through the wreckage smoke drifted up towards the clouds.

Elsdon sat quietly in the veranda. In the bin out back he'd found his book of stories. It had been damaged by potato peelings and tea-leaves but he held it closely to him and stared across the road. The revival tent had already been dismantled and there were some sheep in the paddock now. Elsdon walked across to talk to them. He wanted to go and have a gizzo at the melted sewing-machines but was too scared his mum would give him another hiding. 'You're a wicked, wicked boy, Elsdon,' his mum had told him. 'I haven't forgotten what you said at the meeting. The devil is in you. You are filled with Satan's lust.'

Elsdon held up his hands to show the sheep. 'I got burned in the big fire,' he told them. 'I was trying to be a fireman but I felled down and went to sleep. Mum said I'm filled with Satan's luss. I don't know what Satan's luss is. Not too good, I reckon.'

The sheep stared back at him through the barbed wire. 'A bloke wouldn't credit it,' Elsdon added in his next breath. 'It was a real beaut blaze.'

He sat down on the grass verge and pushed bunches of clover through the fence. The sheep watched but didn't approach. Elsdon's hands were very sore. He was brave, he didn't cry. He had woken up the second night with his fingers throbbing. His mum had found him in the kitchen trying to get a bottle of milk out of the safe. Silently she made him some cocoa and led him back to bed. Uncle Bill had been snoring. 'I don't know what punishment is in store now,' she had told him the day before. 'I've reached the end of my tether. I'm worried sick, Elsdon, worried sick. Your dad will lose his job. We will be forced to leave.'

Elsdon had heard his dad confessing that he'd suspected someone was going to cause trouble. He had received an anonymous note telling him that he was an interfering bloody pom and no one wanted his religion stuffed down their throats.

'You try to be a witness for the Lord and look what they

do,' said Elsdon's mum. 'The Lord is still angered at us, Len. I can't go on.'

The side of the house which faced the factory was badly scorched. Elsdon's mum spent a whole morning scrubbing at it with a bucket of soapy water. As she worked she sang hymns at the top of her voice. She scrubbed until she was bright red in the face. When she came inside she sat on a kitchen chair and wheezed, holding her heart. Elsdon went over to her and tried to hold her hand. With a cry she pushed him away. Elsdon had seen the firemen laughing as they watched her.

None of the factory women had come to work. There was little for them to do, no tidying or cleaning up the mess. Workers from the town council had come and were throwing the blackened rubble into lorries. Elsdon's dad received a letter from the factory owners, up north in the city. The factory was not going to be rebuilt and all the women had been given the boot. Elsdon's dad was told he had to seek another job and that he was expected to give up the house and live elsewhere. The house down Canada Street did not belong to him any more. They held Dad responsible for the fire but, owing to the circumstances, they would not be pressing charges.

Elsdon's dad sat there white-faced and read the letter out loud to Mum late at night. Elsdon was listening from the hall. His mum began to wail and rushed frantically about the kitchen banging the cupboard doors.

Uncle Bill was out the back in the wash-house, even though it was real dark outside. He rarely talked to anyone now and Elsdon had seen him standing beneath the trees down the section staring up into the branches, with a strange look on his face. When Elsdon's mum began making a racket he came in through the back door and shouted at her and his mum burst into tears.

It all began to bother Elsdon. He had no one to talk to about it except the sheep. They had become pretty friendly, coming over to the fence and staring at him while he talked. When he sat silently with the sheep the still, small voice inside his head calmed him a little. 'I reckon one of the heaving women lighted that fire,' he told the sheep. 'Prob'ly didn't like all that preaching. It's enough to make a bloke sick.'

Late one afternoon when his dad came back from helping to clear the rubble his mum told him to go out the back and play. She hadn't said anything about Elsdon rescuing his book of stories from the bin until then.

'You can read your book, Elsdon. You know you like reading it.'

He had taken to walking about with it under his arm.

'Your dad and me need to be on our own,' she said. 'We have things to decide. Sit out in the sun and stay away from the factory.'

Uncle Bill had closed the wash-house door. Elsdon wandered down the section and stared across the fence at the shack where an old Chinaman lived. He would have liked to talk to him but remembered the one in Lower Hutt who might have eaten Snowy. To the right, behind the factory ruins, was an orchard. He went in there and sat beneath one of the apple trees that hadn't been damaged. He opened his book of stories and looked at the pictures.

At the table when he was eating savaloys and tomatoes for tea his mum told him that he would be going to the farm for a few days to stay with Mr and Mrs Smythe-Brown. Elsdon thought his mum had forgotten all about it.

'You can't go back to school yet, Elsdon,' she said, 'because of your sore hands. I told the headmaster. He might give you some lessons to do while you're there. Some sums and social studies.'

Elsdon felt a bit more cheery. He liked the idea of going to the farm. He would take his book of stories and his Meccano set. 'Will there be lots of bulls there?' he asked his mum.

'Cows,' she said. 'It's a dairy farm, Elsdon. You'll get lots of fresh milk and cheese and cream. It will be good for you. Mr Smythe-Brown is a decent Christian man.'

She packed his things into an old cardboard suitcase and gave him two buttered scones wrapped in greaseproof paper the following morning when he was about to leave. Elsdon sat on the concrete at the front and waited for Mr Smythe-Brown to arrive in his truck. Uncle Bill had given Elsdon two shillings for pocket-money but Elsdon didn't know where he'd spend it. 'Are there shops on the farm?' he'd asked his mum.

'Of course there aren't, where's your gumption? You'd better behave when you're there or you'll get a hiding when you get home. I'll hear about it! They won't stand for any of your nonsense.'

'She's pleased to get rid of me, I reckon,' Elsdon told himself as he sat waiting on the concrete. He waved to the sheep in the paddock. 'I'm going to a farm!' he shouted over to them. 'There's some cows there but no sheep!'

'Elsdon!' came his mum's voice from inside the house. 'Stop that racket! Who are you talking to?'

'No one!' Elsdon shouted back.

His mum didn't say anything else.

'Heck, it's hot,' Elsdon said quietly. 'You sheep must feel real sticky with all your wool.' He knew the sheep couldn't hear but he felt a bit bothered sitting there, and needed to talk. 'It'll prob'ly be hot on that farm, but they might have a pond and I could swim. I got my togs in the luggage but I can't swim good. There might be some ducks and I could give them bread and stuff. It's a bit of all right, I reckon, going to this farm. A bloke wouldn't credit it.'

He looked up. His mum was staring at him from a window. She didn't move, just stared at him with a look in her eyes that made him so nervy he squirmed, sitting there. After a long while she moved out of sight. He could still feel her there, inside the house, on the other side of the wall.

When he saw the truck trundling down the street towards the house he jumped up. 'I haven't said tata to Uncle Bill!' he shouted.

Uncle Bill was nowhere to be seen. The wash-house was empty.

'He's having a lie-down,' his mum told him from the kitchen. 'Get your suitcase, Elsdon. Mr Smythe-Brown is waiting.'

Elsdon suddenly didn't want to go. He felt bothered and scared and wanted his mum to hug him. She came out and shooed him along the path. His dad was standing over amongst the factory ruins. Elsdon waved, but his dad just stared.

The ride to the farm in the truck was real exciting. Mr Smythe-Brown drove fast and patted Elsdon on the knee. 'We'll have a grand time of it, mate,' he said cheerfully.

In the back of the truck were two bales of hay and a farm dog. Elsdon tried to pat the dog but it growled at him and showed its teeth.

'It's a working dog,' Mr Smythe-Brown explained. 'Not trained to be friendly.'

By the time they'd reached the farm, rattled over the cow-grid at the gate and along the track to the house, Elsdon had forgotten feeling bothered. Mr Smythe-Brown carried his luggage into the house and Elsdon handed the buttered scones to his wife. 'They were for the trip,' he said, 'but I wasn't hungry, I reckon.'

The few days that Elsdon spent at the farm were perhaps the happiest he had known. Mrs Smythe-Brown clucked over him like a broody chook and he had lots of good things to eat. Elsdon found a kitten in the hayshed and it took to following him about. Because of his bandaged hands he was not expected to help Mr Smythe-Brown, but he did ride on the tractor with him, sitting on the large seat between his legs. Mr Smythe-Brown let him steer the tractor by holding on to his hands at the wrists. Elsdon was taught how to whistle for the farm dogs, which were always running off when needed.

In the evenings they would sit in the front room and play snakes and ladders and I spy. Then Mr Smythe-Brown would read to Elsdon from his book of stories. Elsdon would sit on the floor at his feet and gaze up into his face.

Each morning when Elsdon awoke Mr Smythe-Brown would be already there in the room. He would be kneeling down beside the bed. It made Elsdon feel a bit nervy the first time because it reminded him of his mum doing the same thing. Yet something about these moments was different. He would open his eyes and see a hand reaching out to his face, and at least once, when he was half asleep, he felt his hair being gently stroked. Elsdon began to enjoy the attention.

Elsdon would watch Mr Smythe-Brown playing with the baby. They had a little baby girl whom they loved and cherished. Elsdon discovered jealousy, a sharp pang of feeling in his chest every time Mr Smythe-Brown held the baby to him or jiggled her on his knee. He did not feel excluded, but a slight feeling akin to terror, which he didn't understand.

'He's a bit of all right, I reckon,' Elsdon said to the kitten.

He had called the kitten Snowy, despite its being coal black, and would sit with it in the wooden porch that surrounded the farmhouse. In the porch was a sofa swing where Elsdon would sit after tea, with the kitten on his lap. Sometimes Mr Smythe-Brown would join him there and they would watch the sunset together. Elsdon sat very close to his friend's side. When Mr Smythe-Brown touched him, gave him a rough, awkward hug, Elsdon would tremble. He wanted to ask this man to be his friend, but felt unable to, held back, tongue-tied. 'He must think I'm a bit of a dunce,' he told the kitten when they were alone.

The days passed quietly. Often Mr Smythe-Brown was on the far side of the farm digging holes for fence-posts. Elsdon wanted to go with him but wasn't asked. Mrs Smythe-Brown was usually busy in the kitchen making plum preserves and jam. The kitchen would be full of steam.

On the Sunday Elsdon thought they'd be driving into Morrinsville to the Gospel Hall. Instead they went in the truck to the beach near Waihi for a picnic. It was still dark when Elsdon was woken up.

'It's a long trip, mate,' Mr Smythe-Brown said. 'Mum's cooked up some good grub, and plenty of it. We're a couple of lucky jokers. I've got a bucket in the truck, we can dig for pipis.'

One of the neighbours came to look after Ruth, their little baby girl. Elsdon asked why she wasn't going with them.

'This is your picnic, Elsdon,' he was told. 'Mrs Rawene doesn't mind watching over Ruth. She usually does on Sundays.'

Elsdon sat between them on the front seat of the truck. By the time they left the farm it was sunrise. Elsdon had gone down to the milking-shed and watched Mr Smythe-Brown at work with the cows. Two other blokes were there, helping out. Elsdon wore a pair of gumboots and one of Mr Smythe-Brown's jerseys. A frost had formed during the night and the grass lay covered in white. Elsdon sat on a gate and stared at the men. Every so often Mr Smythe-Brown would look across at Elsdon and grin.

During the journey they played I spy. Elsdon was allowed to score the most points. They drove along back country roads, metal surfaced and dusty. Each of them had to shout to be heard above the racket. Elsdon giggled. Half-way there they pulled into a clearing in the bush and boiled water in the billy for tea. Mr Smythe-Brown gave Elsdon a piggyback when they returned to the truck, and tickled his bare feet.

It was difficult for Elsdon to leave their company after they arrived at the beach. He sat on the blanket in his woollen swimming togs and stared at each of them in turn. 'I'm a bit happy, I reckon,' he said.

They were looking at each other over the top of his head, and grinning.

'Would you like to live with us all the time, Elsdon?' Mr Smythe-Brown asked.

'Oh heck, that'd be real neat, I reckon! I could help on the farm once my sore hands got better. I could milk cows and look after Snowy. If you had some chooks I could mix up mash for them. We had some chooks in Wellington but I wasn't allowed to look after them. I like chooks. Crikey, a bloke wouldn't credit it.'

He looked at each of them eagerly, falling silent when he saw the expressions on their faces. They had stopped grinning. Mrs Smythe-Brown was looking out to sea. Elsdon thought she looked real fed up.

'No worries,' Elsdon said. 'I don't s'pose Mum'd let me anyway. I can come and stay in my holidays.'

When they didn't say anything, he added, 'We could have lots more picnics. Next time I could bring Snowy. I reckon he'd like the beach. He's a bit of all right.'

Elsdon stared at his toes, wiggling them in the fine sand.

'Come on, you lot,' said Mr Smythe-Brown, getting to his feet. 'Let's go and dig for pipis. Last one there will have to boil the billy!'

Elsdon ran as fast as he could.

Each of them had two swims in the outgoing tide. They had dug pipis for an hour, Elsdon finding so many of the shellfish they had to put some back. He helped Mr Smythe-Brown build a huge castle of sand and shells at the water's edge, and afterwards they walked to the rocks at the far end of the beach to peer into rockpools. Mrs Smythe-Brown told them all about sea anemones and crayfish and crabs. As they walked, Elsdon held each of their hands, swinging them back and forth. Elsdon told them all about his lizard, making it into a long story.

'Do you like making up stories, Elsdon?' Mrs Smythe-Brown asked.

'I don't tell fibs,' Elsdon said loudly.

'No, no, of course you don't. I mean would you like to write stories, like the ones in your book?'

'I dunno. Mum reckons I'm not the full quid,' Elsdon told her. 'But I like stories.'

'Perhaps you'll be a writer when you grow up.'

'Better than being a missionary,' Elsdon said, frowning. 'I don't want to go to India. Don't even know where that is.' He looked up into Mrs Smythe-Brown's face. Hers was serious, looking down at him with an expression he had never seen in anyone's face before and wasn't able fully to understand.

Elsdon fell asleep on the way home. He was so tired he didn't wake up even when Mr Smythe-Brown carried him from the truck into the farmhouse and put him to bed, didn't feel the hand which gently stroked his hair, nor the lips which touched his skin. It had been for Elsdon a perfect day.

In the middle of the night he woke up trembling, and

cried out. He had been dreaming. In the dream Mr and Mrs Smythe-Brown were his real parents, he had always been with them here on the farm. Someone had come to take him away, someone faceless, dark and terrifying. He awoke suddenly with a cry so loud that in moments Mrs Smythe-Brown came rushing into the room to comfort him, followed by her husband. They sat on the bed, the kitten in between, and Elsdon clung to them tightly. His small body shook with a fright so real it was a full hour before he returned to sleep. He didn't wake up again until the rooster crowed at dawn. Mr Smythe-Brown was there at his side, reaching out to hug him with his large, roughened hands.

Two days after the picnic there occurred something that was to puzzle and bother Elsdon. He had been awakened early by the kitten, which had climbed in through the open window, jumped on the bed and crawled down beneath the blankets, settling at Elsdon's feet. Elsdon woke up giggling. Snowy had been licking his toes.

Elsdon was peering down at the kitten, the blankets pushed back, when Mr Smythe-Brown came into the room in his shorts and work-boots. Already the day was very hot. 'You're awake early, mate,' he said.

'Yeah, it's pretty hot to sleep,' Elsdon said. 'The kitten comed in the window and climbed in my bed. He's real friendly, I reckon. I call him Snowy because we had one called Snowy who was a big cat and he might've been eaten by a Chinaman. My dad said Snowy got runned over, so I'm not sure. Snowy was my friend. I don't have any friends. I had a friend called Maurice but he went to live at Borstal. Can I come on the tractor with you today?'

Mr Smythe-Brown sat on the edge of the bed. He leaned over and ruffled Elsdon's hair. He didn't speak and Elsdon felt a bit bothered. Mr Smythe-Brown slowly slid his hand down the back of Elsdon's neck, all the while with a look on his face Elsdon felt a little nervy about. The room was very quiet, the only sound was Snowy purring. Mr Smythe-Brown suddenly pulled himself away, and with both hands covered his face. He started to cry. Heavy, loud gasps of noise that scared Elsdon. The bed shook and the kitten stopped purring.

At that moment Mrs Smythe-Brown walked in. 'Your breakfast is on the table,' she said to her husband.

To Elsdon she looked pretty fed up, like she'd looked on the beach. She was staring down at the bed. Mr Smythe-Brown hurried from the room. Elsdon looked at the kitten. It had curled up into a ball and was asleep.

'You'll be going home today, young fellow,' Mrs Smythe-Brown told him quietly. 'Your mum wants you.'

Then she left the room, closing the door.

Elsdon wasn't able to talk to Mr Smythe-Brown again. By mid-morning his things had been packed away into his cardboard suitcase. He'd been told that he couldn't take the kitten home with him.

'Your mum said no, Elsdon. I'm sorry. I talked to her on the telephone when she called. You'd be welcome to take the little tyke if it was up to me. Don't you worry, I'll look after him.'

'He's a bit of all right, I reckon,' Elsdon said.

With Mrs Smythe-Brown's eyes on him he felt real bothered and his face started to get red. She was staring at him in a queer way and Elsdon felt he had done something very wrong but didn't know what it was. She stood there quietly for a while, not saying anything else, then went back to the kitchen. After a few minutes Elsdon could hear raised voices, a shout, and the slam of the back door.

'Your dad's driving out to get you, Elsdon,' Mrs Smythe-Brown told him when he appeared in the kitchen doorway. 'He'll be here soon. I'll give you some jam to take home for your mum.'

After his dad arrived in the Morris Minor, which had been scorched by the fire and kept backfiring, Mr Smythe-Brown still hadn't appeared. Elsdon didn't feel able to ask where he was. His dad shook hands with Mrs Smythe-Brown and they talked quietly for several minutes once Elsdon had got into the car with the luggage. Elsdon watched the kitten. It was sitting on the sofa swing washing its paws in the shadow of the porch roof. Mrs Smythe-Brown came over to the car, put her head through the open window and kissed Elsdon on the forehead. 'Hooray, my young fellow,' she said.

Elsdon waved goodbye to her and baby Ruth and black Snowy as he and his dad drove down the track to the gate. In the distance, on top of the hill where cows were munching grass, he saw a lone figure beside the tractor. Elsdon waved, but the figure did not wave back. Elsdon watched, twisting about in his seat, until he wasn't able to see Mr Smythe-Brown any more.

All the way home they drove in silence. The still, small voice in Elsdon's head seemed very loud in the car. He hadn't heard it on the farm.

The sheep were gone from the paddock across the road. The paddock was empty.

Elsdon's mum had taken to her bed. 'She's a bit tired,' Elsdon's dad explained.

The blackened rubble from the factory fire had all been removed and there was simply a stretch of stained concrete where the building had stood.

In the back porch were three suitcases. Elsdon's dad was

leaving the next morning on the train to Wellington.

'He's going to look for work,' his mum told Elsdon. 'We shall wait here until he sends for us.'

Uncle Bill continued to sit out the back in the wash-house. He had begun to eat his meals there. Elsdon went out twice to talk to him, the first time taking a slice of bread and butter with Mrs Smythe-Brown's jam. Uncle Bill's lips moved, but no sound came out. Elsdon picked up his tobacco-pouch and very carefully rolled a smoke, leaving it beside his uncle. 'He's missing Auntie Vida real bad,' Elsdon told himself. 'He's a bit crook, I reckon.'

Elsdon thought about the days on the farm and Mr Smythe-Brown not saying goodbye, as he lay in bed that night. The thoughts bothered him. He felt all jittery inside.

Elsdon and his mum went to see Dad off on the train. Uncle Bill remained in the wash-house with the door shut. Elsdon helped to carry the luggage and got excited when he saw the steam-engine rumbling along the track to where they waited on the station platform. There were no other people catching the Wellington train. Elsdon's mum began to cry and Dad tried to comfort her. Elsdon stood alone a few feet away and watched. They spoke to each other in quiet, desperate voices and when the porter came out and shouted 'All aboard!' Elsdon's dad grabbed hold of Elsdon and hugged him tightly, not able to speak. He stared down into Elsdon's face, then roughly removed his arms and stepped up into the carriage, not looking back. Elsdon's mum was waving a hanky and making whimpering noises. Elsdon stood very still, his arms held stiffly against his sides. He didn't cry, he was very brave. The train gathered steam and with a shriek began to move away from them, picking up speed. The steam rose up into the morning sky, to join the clouds.

As the train started to turn, Elsdon saw his dad's face peering from the carriage window. He didn't wave, he didn't look at Elsdon, but was staring at his mum.

His mum had stopped crying. She was wiping her eyes with the hanky. She stood there without moving, staring off along the empty tracks. When Elsdon said, 'It's enough to make a bloke sick, all this', she shuddered but wouldn't look down at him. 'No worries, Mum,' Elsdon told her, taking her hand. 'I'll be the man now. You won't have to bust your boiler doing all the work. I'll boil the jug for tea when we get back inside.'

Together, still holding hands, they walked across the rail-tracks towards the house.

9 Leaving

'Stacks on the mill, more on still,' Elsdon was chanting. He was sitting beneath a pohutukawa tree on the far side of the paddock, across the road from the house. He was hiding from his mum, who had given him such a walloping with the razor-strop his dad had left that across his legs were painful, dark-red weals. He'd rubbed dock-leaves across the marks.

He was stacking stones, one on top of the other, the way the other blokes at school often collapsed on each other in a heap, shouting the words 'Stacks on the mill, more on still!'

It was early morning and a mist lay over the paddock. From where he sat he couldn't see the house, and his mum wouldn't be able to see him. She had given him the walloping because she had found him in bed with his lizard. He had been made to let the lizard go. 'Stuff and nonsense, Elsdon!' she had yelled as she beat his legs and bottom. 'Stuff and nonsense, do you hear me?'

Elsdon was pretty brave, he reckoned, and didn't cry.

Since his dad had gone his mum didn't talk about Jesus, except for shouting at Him like she often shouted at Elsdon. She had started to shout at Jesus in the middle of the night and it woke Elsdon up. He slept in his own bed again. Uncle Bill had taken the camp-bed out to the wash-house and slept there. He hadn't come out of the wash-house for three days and it was making his mum real wild.

94

'I'm worrying myself sick,' she kept saying. 'It's turning my mind, Elsdon. I can't go on!'

Sometimes, in the evenings when it was quite dark outside and Elsdon was in his pyjamas sitting at the kitchen table, she would talk to him. Elsdon would ask questions and she would answer.

'Was that dead baby Aunt Melva's?' he asked one evening.

His mum had been scrubbing clothes in the kitchen sink. She rarely went out to the wash-house now and scrubbed everything in the sink. When he asked her that she froze, her face held forward, staring out the window. Elsdon could see her reflection in the glass.

'Aunt Melva was always a bit crook in the head, Elsdon,' she told him in a quiet voice. 'No one knew for sure if the little tyke was hers. It had never been registered.'

'I reckon it was hers. I reckon she kept it up in the attic for donkey's years because it was died and she wanted to keep it safe. Did it have a name?'

His mum shook her head and brushed hair out of her eyes. She began to pound the clothes against the side of the sink.

After a long silence Elsdon said, 'I reckon one of the heaving women lighted that fire at the factory. I heard a lady up the road slinging off at us and saying that they all thought Dad was a pommy holy roller and it was all a bit of a dag, a way of getting rid of him. Do you reckon Dad will come back? Has he runned away? He didn't say hooray to me so I reckon he will come back. A bloke just wouldn't credit it. He's been gone for ages. I s'pose we'll have to pack things and get on that blinking train. Heck, we've got so much stuff it'll bust our boilers carrying it all to the station. It's a bit . . .'

'Elsdon! That's enough, do you hear me?'

His mum's shout was so loud they heard Uncle Bill come

out of the wash-house. He stood in the porch and peered at them through the window, his nose pressed to the glass.

'I reckon Uncle Bill's a bit crook, Mum,' Elsdon continued. 'I saw him having a widdle against the wall of the house the other day, and when I went up to him he asked me who I was. He was acting a bit shickered in my opinion from the beer, and he ponged. I s'pose he misses Auntie Vida and that. Will he come to Wellington when Dad sends for us?'

Elsdon was still talking when his mum belted him across the head with her clenched fist. She hit him so hard Elsdon was thrown from his chair and his glass of milk went with him, shattering on the lino, milk spraying all over him. His mum grabbed his hair and dragged him across the floor, along the hall and shoved him into his room, then stood there and kicked him. She slammed the door shut and locked it. Elsdon lay against the bed. For a few minutes everything was silent. Then his mum began to shout. She was shouting at Jesus. Elsdon put his hands over his ears.

Elsdon tried to talk to his mum many times during those weeks, with often the same, or a similar, result. It was his only way of trying to get close to her. He felt she was going away from him too. She wouldn't let him touch her. He would listen to her from the hall while she talked to someone in the kitchen who wasn't there. She didn't always talk to Jesus. 'It's turning my mind!' she would say. 'I can't go on, it's too much for a body to bear. I've heard nothing from Len, nothing. I don't know where he is, even Mrs Daniels wrote and said she hadn't seen him.'

Elsdon would listen to her singing hymns while she scrubbed the kitchen floor on her hands and knees. The singing would grow louder and louder until Uncle Bill would bang on the back door and shout at her. In the silence Elsdon would creep back to his room and get into bed, pulling the blankets over his head.

He had stopped talking to Jesus. It made him a bit bothered, talking to Him when his mum kept shouting at Him. Like he had done many times, he watched her from the kitchen window, her face turned up to the sky, shaking her fist. 'Leave us alone!' she would shout. 'Haven't you done enough?'

Elsdon didn't know what to do about his mum. She didn't sit down and have tea with him at five o'clock. Some days he would come home from school and find the house empty. Except for Uncle Bill, who'd be shut in the wash-house. Outside the wash-house door were dozens of empty beer bottles. Uncle Bill would make trips to the hotel and bring beer home. Elsdon's mum left his tea and other food on a tray outside the door. Often it went untouched. Neither of them ate much any more.

Elsdon would find his mum down the back of the section. She'd be digging up the grass with a spade and planting veges. There were rows of growing veges everywhere, all over the lawn. Without having to ask, Elsdon reckoned she was growing food for their tea, because there wasn't much money left and his dad sure hadn't sent any. A bloke from the Morrinsville garage had taken away the car and given money for it, so his mum couldn't be really broke. When she came inside she would be breathing painfully, her face red and strained. Elsdon would try to give her a hug, but when he went to put his arms around her she would stand very still, not touching him or hugging him back. Other times she would shove him away, with a deep cry.

It was now two months since his dad had left. Elsdon had taken to sitting under the pohutukawa tree in the paddock most mornings before he went to school, for it was at those times his mum seemed at her worst.

His teacher had begun to examine him, keeping him back at playtime when all the others were sitting in the sun or playing games. Elsdon would offer his teacher a vegemite sandwich from his tin and they would sit there quietly and eat together. Although lately Elsdon's mum forgot to give him anything for lunch. His teacher began to bring enough sandwiches for them both. Elsdon thought it real neat, for inside her sandwiches she would put luncheon meat or cold mutton and she brought fruit, a couple of feijoas, or tree tomatoes. Elsdon loved feijoas.

Elsdon would talk.

'My dad's runned off. He's gone to Wellington to look for a job because the factory got burned. It's enough to make a bloke sick. We aren't too lucky, I reckon. Mum's pretty shook about it. My hands are better, I reckon.'

And he'd hold them out to show his teacher. The bandages had been removed some time ago, but the skin on the back of his fingers was still pink.

'Did they hurt?' his teacher asked.

'Heck, no. I was pretty brave. When we dug for pipis at the beach I used the spade and it didn't hurt. I would have put that blinking fire out too if it hadn't gone all bung.'

His teacher would examine the red weals on his legs, and when asked Elsdon would show her the bruises on his bottom. During the examination she would not say anything. One day she took him by the hand to the headmaster's office and he sat outside on a form and tried to hear what his teacher said. She had made the headmaster look at his legs. Then they shut themselves in and Elsdon couldn't hear what they said, as the door was too thick.

'Mum'll only get real wild if you send any more letters,' he told his teacher when she came out.

'She shouldn't hit you, Elsdon,' his teacher said sternly. 'Whatever the headmaster says. You're a good little chap, Elsdon. You're very clever, do you know that? I always like the stories you write.'

'A lady told me I might be a writer,' Elsdon said. 'That

was Mrs Smythe-Brown,' he added, feeling a bit bothered. He always felt like that when he thought about her and Mr Smythe-Brown.

Mrs Smythe-Brown had come to see his mum one Sunday. She came alone in their truck and didn't enter the house. Elsdon had watched her and his mum through the window and saw his mum get real wild and red in the face. She started to shout, then she cried and Mrs Smythe-Brown left.

'She's not having you, Elsdon. I've told her! She isn't to come here like that, bothering us. It isn't right.'

Elsdon learned that Mr and Mrs Smythe-Brown had had a son, the same age as he was now, who'd died of tuberculosis two years ago. After Elsdon had been there for his holiday Mr Smythe-Brown had written to his mum and dad asking if they could adopt Elsdon.

'It's sinful. They're supposed to be Christians. They can't adopt someone who already has parents. I told her, Elsdon. I told her you wouldn't want to leave your mum. It's shameful. It's part of our punishment. It's judgement.'

Elsdon went to his room and sat on the bed. He held his book of stories and stared out the window at some bulls in a shunter on the other side of the hedge. He felt bothered, wanted to talk to the bulls, but all he could see of them were their poop-covered bottoms. 'I could've been their son,' he said.

With the two shillings that Uncle Bill had given him he bought an exercise-book and two lead pencils. He kept the book and the pencils under the bed with the remainder of the money in a paper bag. He began to take the book and a pencil with him to the base of the pohutukawa tree. He would sit there and write. His English wasn't good but he wrote rather a lot of words about the lizard he'd been forced to let go. He called the lizard Henry. He showed the stories to his teacher and sometimes she read them out in class. Elsdon felt pretty proud. He would sit there listening to his stories, grinning from ear to ear. It made no difference that the blokes in the class added the name sissy to the other names he was called.

'When I get big,' he told some new sheep in the paddock, 'I'm going to be a famous writer, I reckon. I shall write lots of stories and live in a flash house and get shickered on beer when I want to.'

Elsdon did not go to school every day. When his mum had given him a real hard walloping with the razor-strop or had kicked him, she often kept him home. Elsdon had grown to think of his teacher as his friend, and fretted when he wasn't at school. 'It doesn't matter, Elsdon! You're not the full quid anyway. I need you here,' his mum would tell him.

One morning he was still in bed when he heard his mum banging the cupboard doors in the kitchen, rattling pots. When he heard a plate smashing on the floor, Elsdon went out to have a look. His mum was still in her nightie, kneeling on the floor, putting pieces of broken dinner plate into a rubbish bag. On the kitchen table sat a letter. His mum's face was red and swollen. There was damp all down the bottom half of her nightie and Elsdon could smell wee. He went over and helped her pick up the pieces of plate. As he joined her there on the floor she drew herself away, trying to hide the area of wet from him. 'I'm crook, Elsdon,' she said, and began to cry. 'I can't go on. I'm going mental, Elsdon, going mental! It's too much to bear!' And she shook with weeping, rocking her body back and forth, clutching herself.

Elsdon felt pretty nervy and stood up.

'They've told us to leave,' his mum said, pointing to the letter on the table. 'Reckon we've had enough time. They want the house back. We've got to leave!' And she continued to weep, sitting on the floor.

Elsdon put his arms around her head, drawing her to him. She leaned against him. The smell of wee made Elsdon sneeze but he stood there holding his mum and began to stroke her hair, remembering the man stroking his, on the farm. 'No worries, Mum,' he said. 'I'll look after you. We could go to Wellington on the train and look for Dad and he'd pay them for our fares after. He'd be pretty happy to see us, I reckon. A bloke wouldn't credit it.'

His mum had stopped bawling her eyes out but was breathing heavily. Slowly she lifted up her arms and slid them about him. She hugged Elsdon, held him to her, was calmer and quieter now. They remained there together for a long time. Neither saw Uncle Bill staring at them through the window.

Later in the day when Elsdon was sitting at the kitchen table watching cheeky mina birds running across the lawn and pecking at the freshly dug earth, Uncle Bill came out of the wash-house. He knocked several of the beer bottles over and they clinked and rolled down the porch steps. Uncle Bill stared at Elsdon through the glass. Elsdon waved and went to get up out of his chair, but something held him back, and he felt pretty bothered.

Uncle Bill was wearing his pyjama top but not the bottom. He hadn't shaved for a couple of weeks and looked real thin and pale. His face was sunken. He stared at Elsdon and didn't seem to know who he was. Uncle Bill walked down across the grass, then stood in the middle of the dug earth staring up at the sky. After a few minutes he went back into the wash-house and closed the door, not looking at Elsdon again.

Elsdon went out the back and picked the beer bottles up, standing them against the house.

'Ten brown bottles, all against the wall,
Ten brown bottles, all against the wall,
And if one brown bottle should accidentally fall,
There'd be . . .'

He stopped singing the song when his uncle started banging on the wash-house door. Elsdon didn't know the proper words but thought it a good tune and hoped Uncle Bill might've joined in. He remembered their having a singsong once in Wellington.

In the silence that followed, Elsdon sat down on the porch steps and watched the mina birds. They had flown up into the trees when Uncle Bill had appeared but now were running over the grass and earth again. Elsdon looked over his shoulder at the wash-house door. 'Enough to make a joker get shickered,' he said.

His mum was still in bed when he woke up the next morning. Elsdon expected that he would go to school but wasn't keen with his mum acting so crook. Besides, his teacher asked too many questions. His mum had spent half the night banging cupboard doors and moving furniture and singing hymns out loud. At one time she came into his room and took everything out of his tallboy and piled the clothes on the floor. She stopped singing but muttered to herself and kept shaking her fist at the ceiling. Elsdon pretended to be asleep.

She was snoring as he peered through the doorway. Elsdon tiptoed out into the kitchen and found some milk in a jug. He poured it into a glass and drank it, staring out the window. The wash-house door stood open. In the porch there were several folded sheets of paper, a Bible, and an open suitcase filled with clothes neatly folded. The beer bottles were gone.

'Crikey, Dad's come home!' Elsdon shouted.

He shouted the words again, but it didn't wake his mum

as he thought it might. She was still snoring. She had taken to locking the back door before she went to bed. Elsdon rattled it. 'Oh heck, he's prob'ly been shutted out all the night with Uncle Bill,' he said. He found the key and opened the door, and then rushed out to the porch calling 'Dad, Dad, where are you?'

The first place he looked was in the wash-house. Uncle Bill wasn't wearing any clothes. Around his neck was a rope. The rope was tied to the rafters above him. His face was swollen, purple in colour. His tongue was sticking out. There was sick all down his chest and his eyes were wide open. They seemed to be staring at Elsdon. A couple of blowflies were crawling across his lips. Below his feet on its side was the chair on which he'd stood. In the corner of the wash-house was a mattress. The camp-bed lay against the copper boiler, folded up. The wash-house ponged. When Elsdon saw the piles of poop all over the lino he backed out through the door.

He was still standing there, his body shaking, emitting little cries of shock, when he saw his mum peering out the kitchen window. He tried to call out to her, his body shaking so much and his face so hurt his mum rushed out, her gaze at first on his face moving to the suitcase and papers in the porch, then to Uncle Bill's body. She stumbled, let out a long groan, her hands moving up to her face and remaining there. Elsdon grabbed hold of her nightie, pulling at it, needing her to look at him again and give comfort, her groans becoming sharper. She twisted her body, taking hold of Elsdon's arms, wrenching his fingers away from her clothing, and with a strength that filled him with terror she picked him up bodily and threw him from her. Elsdon hit the edge of the porch, landing on his side, his scream of pain so piercing his mum ceased her cries. She ran to him, gathered him into her arms, calling his name over and over again.

The doctor insisted that Elsdon was kept in bed for at least two weeks.

There had been a lot of comings and goings during that time and Elsdon was fussed over a great deal by everyone except his mum. At night-time when they were alone in the house Elsdon would cry out for her, and although he could hear her moving about, she never came to him. He didn't understand why she wouldn't look him in the face when she brought his meals. Her hands would tremble as she laid the tray on his lap, after he'd struggled to sit up. 'I love you, Mum,' he'd say to her. At which she would make a choking noise and leave the room.

Elsdon would eat his tea staring out through the small window. He'd talk to the cows in the shunters outside.

'Mum won't talk. She's feeling pretty shook because Uncle Bill died and Dad hasn't come home. That was Uncle Bill's suitcase in the porch. I thought it was Dad's. Uncle Bill left all his papers and stuff there for Mum so she'd know what to do after he'd done himself in. It's enough to make a bloke sick, all this carrying on. A body can't bear it, I reckon.'

In the night Elsdon would sometimes wake up screaming, having dreamed that a bogy man with a purple face and poop on his legs was chasing him through the house. In the dream he was running from the house across the road to the pohutukawa tree in the paddock but always woke up before he got there.

He had bruised his hip badly, when his mum had thrown him, and his right wrist had been hurt. The doctor had put it in a sling. Elsdon heard the doctor asking his mum questions in the hall. He'd crawled out of bed and listened through the keyhole.

'Elsdon's never been the full quid, Doctor,' his mum

104

said. 'I reckon he was trying to lift his Uncle Bill down and somehow he fell against the tubs. You know how dangerous their edges can be. Elsdon was devoted to his uncle. Poor little tyke. He does try.'

The doctor hadn't said anything more and left pretty quickly.

Elsdon lay in bed and listened to his mum singing hymns in the kitchen. Then she bawled her eyes out, real loud.

The doctor came to see Elsdon every day for a week, and never asked Elsdon what had happened. His mum would act all sloppy then and fuss over him. Elsdon showed the doctor his book of stories.

'Oh yes,' the doctor said, beaming. 'A real good bloke, that Kipling is, son. You have a good book there.'

Elsdon let the doctor see his own stories he kept under the bed. 'I'm going to be a famous writer,' he said, 'when I grow up, I reckon.'

One afternoon Elsdon's teacher came. She brought a package wrapped in brown paper and laid it on Elsdon's bed, within his reach. 'You mustn't open it until I've gone, Elsdon,' she said. 'I can't stay long, have to get back to the school!'

To Elsdon she seemed real nervy. She kept looking over her shoulder towards the door. Before she left she hugged Elsdon. Her face was wet. She tried to grin but her face crumpled and she left the room in a hurry. Before his mum came in Elsdon hid the present under the blankets.

'She's not to come here again, Elsdon, I've told her. You won't be going back to that school before we leave. She's heathen, Elsdon, a fallen woman. She lives with a man she isn't married to. He's old enough to be her dad.'

Elsdon heard them having a row out the back. His

teacher had shouted but Elsdon hadn't been able to hear any of the words.

When his mum went out of the room he drew the package out and opened it. Inside the brown wrapping was a book. *Just So Stories* Elsdon read out. Inside the book's cover his teacher had written *For a brave little man, who might also write one day*, and she had added her name, *Emily Vrogop*. Elsdon reckoned he would keep the book for ever. He sat and held it to him, grinning from ear to ear.

Uncle Bill had left some money. He had stored money in the wash-house inside the suitcase and it was enough for his coffin and a burial and for Elsdon and his mum to travel down to Wellington on the train.

His mum acted pretty differently now, in Elsdon's opinion. She did not touch him, and once he was up and about she spoke politely to him as if he were someone else. Elsdon tried to hug her many times during the weeks before they left Morrinsville but she would pull away, with a look on her face that scared him. He didn't understand the fear he saw in her eyes, but remembered its being there when they lived at Waiwhetu Road.

Uncle Bill had been taken off to the undertaker and kept there. He was going with them on the train to Wellington, inside his coffin, and was to be buried alongside Auntie Vida. A truck had been organized to take some of their furniture. Mum and Elsdon were to travel on the train just as Elsdon's dad had done.

Elsdon began to tell the sheep in the paddock.

'We'll be off on our trip soon. We're going on the blinking train. We haven't heard from Dad, but he'll be there to meet us at the station in Wellington, I reckon. My teacher gave me a book of stories called *Just So Stories* and she wrote in it. This sling will have to be on my arm for

106

donkey's years. Heck, it gets real itchy sometimes and I stick sticks down inside to have a good scratch. The doctor said I'll have it taken off when we're down in Wellington again. My Uncle Bill's dead now. He hanged himself in the wash-house and his tongue was sticking out. He was real crook and missed Auntie Vida. We should've done something for him, I reckon.'

Members from the Gospel Hall had kept away from the house down Canada Street after Elsdon's dad had gone. But since Uncle Bill's suicide they began to visit, and held prayer meetings with Elsdon's mum in the front room. She would cry and they would offer comfort.

One evening when Elsdon was in his room looking at the pictures in his new story-book an old geezer came and stood in the doorway. 'Well, Elsdon,' he said in a booming voice. 'And how is our Lord looking after you? Are you thinking about your salvation? You don't want to be a heathen like your uncle, do you? You're getting to be a big boy now, I'm sure you'll be saved soon.' When Elsdon didn't answer, didn't even look up, he added, 'Would you like me to read you a story?'

Elsdon used some words Maurice had taught him. 'No, you can bloody bugger off out of it, you bastard,' he said.

The old geezer stood there for a moment longer, but Elsdon turned his back.

'S'pose I'll get a walloping now,' Elsdon told the cows outside in the shunter. Yet his mum left him alone, and never mentioned his swearing, as if the old geezer hadn't told her.

When the morning arrived it was raining. A heavy, solid downpour which had been falling all night. 'Blimey,'

107

Elsdon said when he looked out the back. The section was flooded and more water was pouring under the hedge from the railway-yard, which was higher up. There were huge puddles of water reaching up to the porch steps. Elsdon pulled on his gumboots, dressed himself in his oil-skin and hat and stomped about in the puddles, thoroughly enjoying himself. He avoided looking into the wash-house, even though his mum had been in there on her hands and knees scrubbing everything. In the back porch were their suitcases and Mum's hat-box. After a few minutes he saw her through the kitchen window. She was standing at the sink.

Elsdon went back inside, leaving the gumboots and oil-skin in the porch. He was hoping to wear them in the train. 'What time will the train get here, Mum?' he asked.

'We've got plenty of time,' she said. 'Please take off those socks, Elsdon. There's a good boy. They're sopping.'

Before he did so he went across to her and, reaching up, hugged her round the waist. 'I do love you, Mum,' he said.

She kept her hands in the sink where she was washing a cup. She stared at the sling on his arm. 'Do you, Elsdon?' she asked quietly.

When they sat down at the table, and while Elsdon had a bowl of Kornies with hot milk and brown sugar, she said, 'Your uncle was mental, Elsdon. He went mental in the end, like Aunt Melva. It's a terrible sin to take your own life. We're all mental on my side of the family. I see that now. I blamed your dad's family. You'll have to live with that for the rest of your life.'

'Will we see Dad again?' Elsdon asked.

His mum didn't answer. She picked up another cup and smashed it against the side of the sink.

His mum had boiled some savaloys and leeks. That was all there was left in the food safe. For pudding they ate two plums each and drank cups of tea. After lunch they were ready.

The truck had been and gone, taking little. Elsdon's mum was leaving a lot of the furniture behind, even the radio Elsdon loved. 'The Brethren are always in need,' she told him. 'They will take what we leave.'

Elsdon had hidden his books and the Meccano set beneath his clothes in the cardboard suitcase. As it was still raining lightly, he was allowed to wear the oilskin and hat and gumboots. Beneath it all he seemed to disappear.

Carrying the luggage between them, watched by the porter who made no attempt to come out of his office and help, they struggled across the front lawn, on to the metal-surfaced road and into the station-yard, up the ramp to shelter beneath the platform overhang.

'Boy,' Elsdon said, out of breath. 'This'll really bust our boilers if we're not careful.'

His mum was wheezing loudly, her face red and strained. Tears ran down her cheeks. She didn't once look back at the house.

They stood alone on the station platform, Elsdon and his mum, surrounded by their luggage. At the other end, sitting on two sawhorses, was Uncle Bill's coffin. Elsdon felt too bothered to go near it. He held on tightly to his mum's hand.

No one had come to see them off. Elsdon had hoped his teacher might come, or the big man from the Dairy Milk Bar, whom he'd gone to say tata to and then left a note for because he wasn't there. None of the Brethren from the Gospel Hall had turned up. Elsdon thought that was pretty mean, seeing they were getting lots of stuff from them.

Elsdon commenced to sing loudly his own version of a hymn.

'Jesus loves us, this I know,
For our Bible tells me so!'

Across the road the sheep in the paddock were gathered beneath the pohutukawa tree. They raised their heads and stared when the singing broke the silence.

After a while, Elsdon's mum started singing too, as the rain ceased to fall and the sun came out. Far to the left, from where the train was approaching, a rainbow began to appear in the sky.

Redemption

Elsdon was sitting on the bread-bin below the tiny kitchen window, staring out. It was his favourite place in the flat and he would sit there for hours talking to his friend Jesus and looking to the right, down the road towards Wellington harbour. Rain was bucketing down and the wind scared him a bit because it made shrieking noises. It was nearly dark. His mum hadn't come home yet. Elsdon watched out for her, and as usual his legs trembled because he had become certain that one day she'd just push off like his dad and leave him all on his own.

'She's at the end of the rope, I reckon,' Elsdon said loudly. 'Crikey, Jesus, you're no help. You listen all right but you haven't done anything. It's enough to make a bloke sick.' And he peered up towards the sky, pulling a face.

They had been living in the poky, run-down flat above Wellington city for donkey's years, in Elsdon's opinion. He went to school not far off but hadn't made any friends there. His mum had worked in four different factories for a few months, each time not able to hold down her job. She'd told Elsdon she was being given money now from the Government and that they'd have to scrimp, there'd be no shouts, no lollies for him and no new clothes. Elsdon reckoned that it was pretty neat of the Government to give his mum a few bob. 'I'm at the end of my rope!' his mum kept on shouting at him.

Uncle Bill had been buried in the cemetery beside Auntie

111

Vida. The funeral was held only a few days after their return to Wellington. Elsdon had not been allowed to go to the service with his mum, who had locked him in when she left the flat. Elsdon wasn't too certain what a funeral involved, as no one had ever told him. He'd always reckoned it was pretty queer, putting someone beneath the sod once they'd died. 'Is it like planting spuds? Will something grow there?' he'd asked several days after the service.

His mum hadn't answered. She had rushed straight across to where he stood and belted him across the head with her fist, knocking him against a table. Later on she shouted, 'You're wicked, do you hear me? You've been filled with Satan ever since you took up with that Maurice. I won't have it, do you hear?'

His mum stared at him with a hatred in her face that made him tremble, and when she wasn't about he could still see her face inside his head. His mum now came into his room in the middle of the night as she'd done in Morrinsville and just stood there in the dark, staring across at him, muttering, while Elsdon lay very still, pretending to sleep. Several times when that happened he'd wet the bed. In the morning she would belt his legs and bottom while she yelled at him about the mess, until he managed to get dressed and run off, to sit on a bench before school. So far, his class teacher hadn't taken much notice of him. The teacher was a real rough bloke with a bushy beard. Elsdon had learned to sit at the back of class and look small. It was a huge school, with dozens and dozens of kiddies. Elsdon kept getting lost. He'd never been given the belt, though. Some of the others in the school were real rude bodgies, in Elsdon's opinion. They were often given the belt for something they'd done wrong. Most of them seemed to hate school. Elsdon was often treated as if he weren't there. He didn't reckon this was too bad.

'It's a bit of all right, I reckon, Jesus,' he sometimes told his friend. 'I've enough on my blinking plate and now I'm getting to the end of the rope like Mum. You wouldn't credit it.'

His mum never visited Uncle Bill's and Auntie Vida's graves after the funeral was over. She never mentioned Uncle Bill again, and she wouldn't let Elsdon speak his name either just as she'd tried to stop him from talking or asking questions about Jesus and Aunt Melva. She didn't contact anyone they'd known before in Wellington.

After they had been back in Wellington for only a few weeks, they had walked holding hands along the city streets, Willis Street and Lambton Quay and down at the docks, looking for Elsdon's dad, his mum carrying a photograph of Len and sometimes stopping people to ask if they had seen him. No one had heard of Len Bird. She told Elsdon she wouldn't go to the coppers when some bloke had suggested it. 'Your dad isn't a crook, Elsdon. I shan't ask the police. We'll find him, he's just got a bit lost somewhere, son. He'll turn up soon.'

His mum had seemed quite cheery back then, in those first few weeks. She had found them the flat straight off and they'd moved in after two nights at a private hotel, which had cost a bomb. She had used some of the money Uncle Bill had left for his funeral.

The flat was on a long, steep hill road called Motions Drive, beside a bush-filled gully, not far from the zoo. It had one purple-painted room and another painted bright orange. There were only a few very small windows in the rooms. The bloke who'd rented out the flat told Elsdon he thought his mum was a real snazzy-looking sheila and that he might ask her out. The landlord was an Aussie. He swore a lot and picked his nose when he thought no one was watching. Most of the time he left them alone, and he came only once a week for the rent. The flat when they

113

shifted in had mice-poop all over the floor and the bath was cracked and slaters crawled up the drain into it. The whole place stank of old poo, but Elsdon didn't say anything. They'd cleaned it up a bit as best they could. Elsdon had scrubbed the walls with water and Jeyes' Fluid.

All that seemed a long time ago now to Elsdon, which it was. Morrinsville was just a memory. They had found no trace at all of Elsdon's dad, and even after his mum had put an advertisement in the *Herald* there'd been no response. Elsdon reckoned his dad was probably hiding from them and was too scared to come out. At the back of his exercise-book he wrote down the names of places where he reckoned his dad could be hiding. Elsdon didn't write any more stories. He felt too nervy. Eventually, when his mum found her first job and began to work, she stopped looking, and for a time it seemed as if everything might be all right. But the work proved too much for her, and she came home more and more often looking pale and crook and acting angry, until one day she just didn't go out to work again, but sat at home moaning and weeping and singing hymns. And after a while she began to go off out alone, telling Elsdon that now the Government supported her she would look for his dad herself, she didn't want Elsdon with her.

One freezing winter night when Elsdon was tucked up in bed reading his book about the little boy brought up by animals, his mum entered his room and stood there glaring. In a deep, dreadful whisper she said, 'Len was all I ever had, he was all I ever loved. I never wanted you. You've ruined my life, do you know that? Ruined it!' And she left the room, closing the door quietly behind her.

After that it all began to crack. Elsdon was a bit older now, he had seen things happen that still made him cry out in the dark, and those bogy men he had once feared were now all round them, staring and muttering and filling Elsdon's dreams with terror. As in Morrinsville, he reckoned he might become loony as well.

His mum began to stop talking to him for long periods after she had whispered those words about her life being ruined. She glared at Elsdon as if she truly hated him, he reckoned. And to prove it, some nights she came into his room and belted him so violently with her fists that he'd feel everything inside his head go black. In the morning he'd wake up and reckon he'd had a real scary dream until he saw the marks on his body and the dried blood and his snot on the sheets. Those nights became a part of their life inside the flat.

There was no one he could talk to about it. Jesus didn't take a blind bit of notice. There was no one at school and the neighbours were too snooty. Yet he still talked to Jesus as he sat on the bread-bin below the kitchen window, peering out after he came home from school.

'Mum hates me now, Jesus. Dunno why. I s'pose it's because Dad's buggered off for good, I reckon. Bloody bastard,' he would add, imitating Maurice. 'It's enough to make a joker crook. I'm getting at the end of the rope. If Mrs Daniels was here, she'd put a stop to Mum, I reckon.'

And Elsdon would cry, getting into a paddy and kicking at the wall, clutching his *Radio Fun* annual and a grader he'd made from the Meccano he couldn't bear to dismantle, while about him the flat would darken, as the night outside the window came inside.

One morning before dawn Elsdon woke up, having heard what he reckoned was his mum shrieking his dad's name. He lay very still, but the flat was quiet and even the rain which usually made a heck of a racket had stopped falling.

Then from outside his door he could hear a strange sound of breathing. For a moment he couldn't move. When the sound stopped he crept out of his bed, pulled on his dressing-gown, and tiptoed to the door. He opened it and peered out. At first he couldn't see much, for his eyes were bunged up with the yellow paste he often found in them in the morning. When his sight cleared he moved out into the tiny, windowless hall.

His mum was standing in the open doorway that led to the kitchen. She was in the nuddy and held her arms straight out from her sides, staring intently past Elsdon to the far end of the hall. On her face Elsdon could see a queer grin, which made her teeth shine in the dark. When she didn't move, Elsdon squinted towards what she was looking at, but there was no one else in the hall and nothing to see. The walls were bare. 'Crikey, she's real crook this time,' Elsdon whispered to himself.

He went to step back into his room feeling real nervy, but the sudden movement caused his mum to cry out and she looked straight at him. 'Len! Oh Len, you've come, I knew it, you're here. You've come home!' And as she cried out she rushed towards Elsdon, grabbing his shoulders and pulling him to her. She crushed Elsdon's face against her breasts and he began to gag when the smell of wee got up his nose. It was overpowering.

He struggled as best he could, starting to whimper, but his mum held on for dear life, squeezing his arms until he shouted out in pain as her fingernails gouged into his skin. 'Len! Len! Len!' his mum shrieked.

With one big heave Elsdon pulled himself from her, only to look up and see her eyes like those of the worst bogy man he had ever dreamed of staring down at him. He was filled with a terror he had never known before. He scurried backwards, hitting the frame of his door and almost falling, but his mum came after him now, the fury in her face causing Elsdon to cry out her name. But that had no effect. When she grabbed hold of him again, she began belting him across the head, trying to bite at his face at the same time, and Elsdon started screaming, hitting out with his fists.

Suddenly she went still and just stood there glaring at Elsdon as if she didn't fully know who he was or what she'd been doing. After a long moment of silence she fell to the floor at Elsdon's feet and lay motionless, her face hidden by her hair.

'Oh heck, she's dead, she's dead,' Elsdon whispered. He knelt down and reached for her arm, holding it tightly just as she opened her eyes, moving her head slowly towards him, her breath rattling and wheezing.

Elsdon helped her back to bed. She was gasping for breath and weeping loudly. Her face looked purple.

'No worries, Mum,' Elsdon told her. 'You're feeling real crook, I reckon. It's enough to make a bloke go out and get shickered. I'll look after you, don't you fret. I could go and look for Dad, the bugger. I know places to look, I reckon. I'd find him. You stay in bed, you're at the end of the rope.'

As soon as Elsdon had tucked her into bed she fell asleep. He tiptoed from the room. Later he took in a lighted candle in a holder and placed it beside her bed.

In the morning she was up, making Elsdon's breakfast as usual, and she even grinned at him over her shoulder from where she stood at the oven. She was cooking eggs. 'You need feeding up, Len!' she said brightly, but she stared at Elsdon for such a long time he felt real nervy sitting at the table. She reckoned he was his dad come home.

After that his mum wouldn't speak to him at all. She banged all the pots and pans and when she dropped a half-full milk bottle on the floor she simply walked over the pieces. Elsdon watched the milk dripping from her nightie where it had splashed. She didn't clean up the mess. Her lips were moving as if she were yacking nineteen to the dozen. But no sounds came out. After breakfast when he left the flat to go off to school she was on her knees scrubbing the hall floor. And when he said 'Tata, Mum' she raised her head and, taking hold of the bucket she was using, she crashed it down on to the floor. There was no water in the bucket.

As those days and nights slowly passed by, there grew between Elsdon and his mum a silence and a fear that Elsdon did not know how to cope with. Sometimes he talked to his friend Jesus even when his mum was in the same room. He talked to Jesus as if he were talking to his mum, hoping that she might be listening. 'Now this blinking rain's stopped I could get out after school, Jesus,' he'd say. 'I could go and look for Aunt Melva's house, I reckon, and see what it's like now. There might be someone there who'd help. I could get on the train and go to see Mrs Daniels. Crikey, she'd be real shook to see me. I'd tell her you don't do anything to help, you blinking bugger.'

He would look at his mum for a response, using the swear-words he had learned from Maurice. She had taken to sitting on her chair facing the wall when she wasn't moving about. Sometimes Elsdon would go to her and hold her, give her a hug. Once, she moved her head sharply and bit him on the arm.

She'd begun to pong. Elsdon kept fretting as to whether he should give her a bath but wasn't certain how to go about it. Whenever he talked directly to her she would lift up her hands and cover her face until he stopped. Sometimes she held her hands over her face for a long time. During the night Elsdon began to lie awake listening to her walking about the flat, weeping loudly and some nights shrieking out his dad's name. She did not enter his room.

118

Elsdon kept a chair pushed against the door, angled beneath the door-handle.

Elsdon dawdled on the way home from school. He had discovered the Wellington Zoo and would stare across the high boundary fence by climbing a tree that stood down the side of a gully. On the other side of the fence was a paddock where there lived an old rust-coloured bull with queer horns and enormous eyes.

'I bet you like it in there!' Elsdon shouted out to the bull one afternoon. 'I'd like to live in there too, I reckon! My mum's got a bit loony now and I'm looking after her. We had bulls in Morrinsville but they didn't have huge horns like you. And they weren't lucky, I reckon. They were made into meat, so I didn't know them much! Oh well, I got to go now and cook Mum's tea. She's not eating much, but I'm a pretty neat cook. When I grow up I'll cook and write stories every night and get famous and go to England where the poms are. They're neat. A bloke wouldn't credit it!'

When he stopped shouting he felt a bit sick. As he watched for a while longer the bull did a huge poop. There were two ladies staring at the bull from inside the zoo. They were grinning like real loonies. One of them was sucking a red ice-block.

Usually when he let himself into the flat after school his mum would be in bed, so Elsdon had taught himself how to cook sausages and heat up tinned food, boil veges. Today, with the sun having been out for most of the afternoon, Elsdon cheery after his talk with the bull, the flat itself seemed pretty bright and cheery. There was a restful silence and a sound of cicadas from out the back where there grew a spread of bush. He went straight to his room and left his satchel on the bed. When he looked into his mum's room the bed was empty. The room was very tidy and clean, and bare. There were no clothes lying about. His mum's suitcases were gone from the top of the wardrobe. Elsdon felt his heart thump like anything and his mouth went dry. He held his tinker with both hands, suddenly wanting a pee. 'Crikey,' he whispered. 'She's pushed off, I reckon.'

His mum was at the table in the kitchen. Surrounding her on the floor were her suitcases, both of which were packed up, bits of clothing poking out from where she hadn't tucked them in properly. Her two hat-boxes were beside the chair where she was sitting. On the table in front of her sat two cardboard shoe-boxes, opened, which were overflowing with papers and letters and old photographs. His mum was leaning forward with her face resting on the table surface, and her eyes were open, staring straight at Elsdon when he entered the room.

She was dead.

Elsdon was pretty brave, he reckoned. He didn't cry, though he felt a bit nervy. His mum's eyes seemed to follow him while he moved about the kitchen pouring milk from a bottle on the sink and fetching the biscuit tin. He sat down at the table and reached out to hold one of her hands which were resting loosely in her lap. He leaned down and peered closely into her eyes, touching them gently and, with great concentration, he traced the dark-blue veins that lay just below the surface of her skin. Her eyes were cloudy, as if the tears that had been in them had changed colour. Her mouth was open. His mum's hand was cold, but he held on to it for dear life, and talked to her.

'Oh yeah, you're here, Mum. I've got back from school. I went to look at the zoo. They've got this big old bull there, he looked just like that big man at the Dairy Milk Bar at Morrinsville.'

Elsdon giggled, then he stopped, biting his tongue.

'I reckon you'll be up in that Heaven now with Uncle Bill and Aunt Melva and Auntie Vida. Crikey, you're all up there except Dad, the blinking bugger. A bloke wouldn't credit it.'

He stared into the shoe-boxes. On the top of one sat a grubby, creased envelope with his name *Elsdon Bird* and the words *My Nephew* scrawled across it in what Elsdon reckoned was real juddery handwriting. He couldn't take his eyes off the envelope, for he reckoned he knew who the letter was from. Uncle Bill. His mum must have kept it hidden all this time, ever since his uncle had done himself in. Yet he couldn't pick the letter up, as much as he wanted to. He just sat there at the table holding his mum's hand until it was completely dark outside and he could see a full moon and hundreds of stars and heard the whistling of the wind.

It was nearly dawn when Elsdon got up from his chair. He was shivering with cold. He had cried for a bit and the snot from his nose had dried across his lips. He wiped them with his fists. For a large part of the night he had talked and talked to his mum and it had not made him sick, as his talking often had, but gave him a feeling like being a little bit happy. He had told his mum that he loved her and reckoned she had heard.

Walking very slowly through the flat to his bedroom he found his oilskin and hat and gumboots stored at the back of his wardrobe. He hadn't worn them since he and mum had left Morrinsville in the train, despite all the rain falling here in the big smoke. After he'd pulled the oilskin on and put on the hat and the gumboots, he seemed to disappear beneath it all. The oilskin had always been too big for him. It had belonged to his dad.

Back in the kitchen he stood beside the table and stroked

his mum's hair, patting it smooth. He hugged her, and kissed her on the cheek. 'No worries, Mum,' he said quietly.

He reached out to take the letter with his name on it from the shoe-box, but when he touched the envelope he quickly drew his hand back as if it had been scorched. For one brief moment he felt that someone else was in the room with him and his mum. But he was very brave. He picked up the envelope and then ran through into the hall and out the front door, down the path, not looking back.

Outside, a heavy frost lay on the earth. There was no wind, not one cloud to be seen. The sky was growing pale with light as the sun began to rise. Elsdon closed the paling gate that led into the yard. He stared up at the windows of the flat. 'No worries, Mum. Don't you worry a flaming bugger about anything!' he shouted as loudly as he could. 'I'm off now!' he added, after a few minutes. Yet he still stood there, hidden beneath the oilskin and hat, peering up at the windows, unable to move away. He knew that his mum was dead, for he had felt her get colder and colder as the night had moved on and her hand had become real stiff and he wasn't a drongo, he reckoned. He'd known straight off when he'd come home from school and seen her. But he was pretty shook about leaving her all on her own and he started to cry, looking up and down the road. The houses were dark, the people in them still sleeping.

After a while he stopped crying and rubbed the back of his hand over his nose while he listened. Then, turning away from the gate, marching down along the middle of the road swinging his arms, his eyes brightening with the new day, Elsdon Bird set off towards the awakening city below.